THE
CITY OF
FOLDING FACES

Jayinee Basu

LANTERNFISH PRESS

PHILADELPHIA

THE CITY OF FOLDING FACES
Copyright © 2019 by Jayinee Basu

Lanternfish Press
399 Market Street, Suite 360
Philadelphia, PA 19106
lanternfishpress.com

Cover Design by Mallory Grigg
Cover Image © 2019 Getty Images/wundervisuals

Printed in the United States of America.
Library of Congress Control Number: 2018959586
ISBN: 978-1-941360-26-2
Digital ISBN: 978-1-941360-27-9

for Patrick

THE
CITY OF
FOLDING FACES

Jayinee Basu

PART I

Mara was underwater: suspended and swaying marinely in a light green broth of plant matter, her body getting progressively lighter, nearly floating off the slippery plastic seat of the chair. The water felt cool around her face as her eyelids drooped. Everything was silent except the muffled glubbing of her heart. Eventually a flutish tone sounded, followed by a male speech emulator.

Welcome to the GUA Lab. GUA is an abbreviation for Graphic Understanding of Affect, a tool for visually recording the interaction between facial affect and neurotransmitter activity. The GUA Lab is dedicated to furthering scientific and cultural understanding of Ruga people, and to facilitating research on the special medical needs of this population. In order to map the vastly increased quantity of affect in the Ruga, the GUA Lab has designed a test, also called GUA, that you are about to take. The technicians to your right will be operating the GUA device. Please take a seat.

In front of you is a high-frame-rate camera that will take five thousand images of your face every second. When instructed, please straighten your back and lean into the vertical backrest. Your head will be held in place from the sides by two metal clamps. These clamps will stabilize your head for a series of cisternal punctures that will occur at the base of the skull. A microdialysis probe will be inserted into these punctures.

It is very important to remain absolutely still during this process. There is moderate-to-severe pain associated with this portion of the test. Since chemical anesthetics disrupt the recording, we have projected a virtual reality environment of a lake for you to inhabit during this process. Prior subjects have found the environment to provide a measure of pain relief. Once this process is done, you may rest.

We at the GUA Lab thank you for your service to science.

Mara nearly fell asleep during this announcement despite her anxiety and the metal clamps that gripped her scalp like a giant spider. A robot applied cold antiseptic solution in a circular massaging motion at the back of her neck, further lulling her toward sleep. An excruciating pain at the same spot jolted her back and she stifled a scream. To her right, a holographic shape began to glow.

The abalone-colored projection was a cube with half the faces removed to expose the three internal axes. Made of an ambiguous material textured like cloth, the hemicube had bulges and ripples and threaded articulations embroidered throughout. Undulating in the watery atmosphere, it appeared anemone-like: an alien life-form unmoored.

Mara tried to look at it without moving her head. Despite her efforts, a nearly imperceptible flexion of her neck caused an electric jolt to discharge down her spinal cord, sending waves of pain sweeping through her body. She closed her eyes and focused on breathing in and out through her nose.

Please repeat: 2 + 3 = 5, said the male speech emulator.

Mara croaked the phrase and saw something tiny begin to grow inside the cube from the very edges of her perception. The act of speaking had released an entirely new type of agony located somewhere near her temples.

Please repeat: 2 + 2 = 5.

"2 + 2 = 5," Mara said, and sensed the tiny thing grow or move somehow in response.

Please express outrage.

"Um," Mara said. She had not been warned about this.

Please express outrage, the speech emulator insisted after several seconds.

Mara rummaged within herself for such a feeling but was unable to locate it.

Please express outrage, the speech emulator said for a third time.

"How dare you?" Mara offered weakly.

The emulator seemed satisfied, but only momentarily.

Please produce a lie of omission.

It went on like this for some time.

By the end of the test twenty minutes later, Mara had started panting with her tongue out like a dog. The hemicube now contained a beautiful, tangled mass of what appeared to be glowing lavender aerosolized string that continued to grow at one end, synchronized with the throbbing pain that would become Mara's entire universe for the weeks that followed.

The technician turned off the virtual reality environment. Mara felt her body drop back into the chair.

The needle was replaced by the robot massaging the puncture wound with antiseptic. It placed a bandage over the hole and taped it shut. Mara's lip trembled as she tried not to weep. Endorphins tumbled through her body. The tube lights in the room sparkled aggressively.

"And that's it. You did great. How do you feel?"

Mara blinked the water away from her eyes. The metal clamps released with a light whirr. She didn't dare turn her head.

"I'm sure you're still sore, but it's good to get in the habit of moving your head. If I may?"

The technician stood in front of Mara and gently held her head, thumbs at her chin, with both hands. He then moved her head ever so slightly to the right. Pain radiated from the puncture wound in roiling curls. Mara whimpered.

"I'm sorry," the technician said, and released her head. He informed her that he had already sent a prescription for the strongest narcotics indicated for her post-procedure care to the pharmacy; that she was welcome to rest for as long as she needed; and that her results would be sent to her within the week. As he asked whether someone was coming to pick Mara up and thanked her for her service to science, she trembled in the chair and watched her pain twist in combed currents through the air of the room.

———

An explosion in new math enabling people to access the equation that determines their space-time tubeform has given rise to a subculture known as Ruga, wherein individuals who learn their equation are affected with chronic derealization resulting in dimensional dysphoria. This condition is referred to as Post-Roulette Syndrome, named after the Casino-developed portal through which the equation can be accessed. For such people, traversing four-dimensional space-time is disorienting. They report a radical augmentation in the complexity of their perceptions and emotions, and an accompanying distress at the difficulty in communicating these nonstandard affects with standard human facial muscles and vocal tracts. Fortunately, breakthrough research has relieved these individuals of the former complaint, and steps are being taken to address the latter.

The field of designer wrinkles started out with algorithms for creating realistic cloth on-screen but has now splintered into the research and development of custom expressions. For most of human history, facial expressions have been communicated with the same group of muscles conserved within mammals for millions of years. However, new math in the ruga mechanics of creasing has led to the development of body modification surgeries allowing facial muscles to crumple into elaborate and infinitesimally small folds and wrinkles.

The Ruga do not experience or portray human emotions in the same way as other people. When a Ruga person encounters a happy stimulus, for example, she does not smile. Instead, a filigreed map might emerge from the skin of her forehead like a hyper-detailed silicone subdermal implant with shapes that communicate not just happy but perhaps also sorrow, and pinkish, and an acknowledgment of the fleeting nature of happiness. To be clear, the shapes are not produced by an implant but by the individual's own vascular system and musculature. Through a mechanism that is not as of yet well understood, the patterns are thought to correspond to the individual's own memories encoded in the cellular substrate of the nervous system. Experimentation with similar manipulations in the larynx and phonatory muscles have shown early promise in the ability to produce novel complexity within utterances as well.

For many non-Ruga people, decoding fractal expressions of emotion is a difficult task. This has led to widespread mistrust and social alienation of folks who choose to undergo expression surgery. Further complicating the psychosocial *consequences of the surgery is the apparent side effect of some Ruga individuals losing the capacity to dream. To be precise, it is not that the individuals lose the capacity to remember their dreams but that they indeed cease to undergo REM sleep altogether. While prior research had concluded that REM sleep is important but not essential for normal functioning, in the Ruga its loss leads to a host of learning and mood disorders, the onset of which can be subtle yet profound. Importantly, Ruga individuals are no longer capable of synaptic pruning. This, in turn, leads to massively increased computational entropy, as well as global memory encoding and retrieval issues.*

While some Ruga people view this aspect of their new identity as prohibitively intrusive in their day-to-day lives, others welcome it. A shorter memory span results in hyperdynamic and ever-changing forms of expression, resulting in a life lived in a constant state of astonishment.

Mara leaned closer to the article to inspect a grainy image of a globe-shaped machine. Two rows of smiling scientists stood before it, some wearing dark blue T-shirts with white letters spelling out CASINO under their white coats. Though it was hard to be sure, they all appeared young and attractive. One scientist had long green hair down to her waist, while another had a large afro that was interrupted by the border of the photo.

Mara turned in a semicircle on her heels away from the printout on the wall, which was sandwiched between two sheets of glass like a three-star review of a diner. Shuffling back to the seating area in the waiting room—careful not to turn her neck—she sat down stiffly on a coffee-colored sofa. It made an assortment of fussy noises. Mara picked at its shiny leather surface in retaliation and boredom. The ride-share car she had ordered from her phone was taking its time, probably stuck in rush-hour traffic. Various parts of her digestive system were conversing in grumbling tones.

From somewhere high above her in the throat of the building, she could hear the cheerful metallic sounds of slot machines. And behind that, what sounded like the voices of birds speaking in human tongues.

———

Arlo was sitting in front of the bay windows of their bedroom, sunlight pouring through his blond curls and marbling his golden skin. He had just finished breaking up with her. Arlo's hands were clasped at his knees and he was looking down at the ground, saying nothing. Mara's grief was overshadowed by an acute bitterness, which seemed to enhance her senses. She could see all the minute ridges of his face—each and every one of the delicate bones. Sunlight glanced off the white tips of his blond eyelashes. Nothing safe and warm could last. The bitterness seemed to be multiplying, as if she were accessing a memory of it over and over and over again. In her head a voice echoed deafeningly while she looked at Arlo's illuminated form.

I wear a string of beads for every period marked by association with another individual. The beads swell in the middle during our aliasing and shrink at each edge during our rupture. Passionate affairs are bulbous, blooming and extinguishing rapidly. Longer friendships are cylindrical, the shape of a lifetime of shared cigarettes.

I am two beings. In the first state, I am covetous and shivering. In the second, I am tall and nurturing. In the first state, I am sensitive to my past digressions. In the second, I have no past or future. In the first state, I am female. In the second, I lack sex. These are not internal truths but external indices. In the first state, I smile and laugh. In the second, I grimace. In the first state, I synthesize. In the second, I manifest. In the first, I am Arnold's cat. In the second, I am

∭∭∭∭∭∭∭∭∭∭∭∭∭∭∭∭. These transformations are consensual.

That our history is a story is a lie we keep being told. It has a shape, yes, but that shape has no more order or meaning than does a clump of hair in a shower drain. At best it is a flickering recollection of sensations haphazardly linked, catalogued and stored for eventual dissolution.

Mara opened her eyes. She was cuddled up to Arlo's chest in bed—the sun was barely up. Arlo's hair was not blond but light brown, his skin creamy but less supernaturally lit than it had been a moment ago. A sense of relief spread through her body when she realized she had awoken from a very brief but very realistic dream. She was, in fact, safe and warm under the blankets next to her boyfriend, who had not broken up with her. She licked her lips and drifted back into sleep.

The experience of paranoia was so subtle for her as to be missed completely. Mara's trust held another person inside of her like cotton ties holding a duvet inside of a cover. During periods of internal roughness, such as during withdrawal from prolonged stimulation, the ties would become loosened, and unless she took great care to retie them by reminding herself of the inherent goodness of people, they would eventually become undone, and the other person would slip out quietly from her heart and accumulate stains for months at the foot of the bed. There would be a period of coldness then, followed by an immediate and complete separation.

Mara shivered in her sleep and drew closer to the warm body next to her as inklings of something being wrong dripped deep into her subconscious, slowly coalescing into a black cloud to be later released in a moment of panic.

———

Mara heard the explosion from the other room. She grabbed her beer and ran into the kitchen, ready to splash it onto whatever was on fire. There was no fire, but the window into the microwave was now yellow. The egg had exploded. Mara scraped the egg off the microwave window onto her plate and ate it. She then re-scraped the microwave, mixed the last remnants of the egg with a little water, and ate that doused with hot sauce. She opened another beer and drank the whole thing, along with one of her pain pills.

Mara locked her doors and headed to the Casino. It

was the day after Christmas, and no one buys expensive baby clothes the day after Christmas, her boss had texted her. Take the day off.

Inside the Casino, Roulette was already in motion. The massive grid of screens was tuned to various channels of gray snow effervescing with intermittent rainbows. Sometimes shapes flickered in and out. A child was screaming *Mommy!* at a particular screen. Mara felt flushed and for a moment her body forgot whether it needed to inhale or exhale. The red plastic walls of the Casino glistened. The spiky fronds of greenery lining the room seemed to stiffen into spears. She steeled herself for a rush of memory.

Nothing rushed. Remembrances did not trickle or drip into the staging area of her consciousness. There was no fog or haze or condensation to speak of except the visible clumps of smoke emitted by patrons in ill-fitting T-shirts who spent their days mechanically pressing levers for coins. Though the smoke and flashing lights of the Casino made her feel light-headed, Mara found herself returning to it several times a week just to walk around, look at the people, and sometimes touch the plastic walls with her fingertips. She felt stuck in a precarious time, the parolee of an internal prison readjusting to freedom.

The child screamed *Mommy!* again and smacked a little hand on the distorted image of a woman as it flashed quickly by, her face pulled toward the corner of the screen. How many transformations had occurred already?

"Ma'am, please secure your child from the screen," a bored voice said over the loudspeaker. Mara looked around for the child's mother. The child howled and slapped the screen once more.

"Ma'am, please secure your child or we will have to ask you to leave the Casino," the voice repeated. Mara realized that it was talking to her. She spun slowly, peering into corners of the room for a camera, pointing at the child and making big X gestures with her arms. *NOT MINE*, she mouthed. An old woman was hurrying toward her.

"Look—" Mara began, but the woman brushed past her and picked up the child. The little girl shrieked and received a slap across the face.

"Her momma's been stuck in there for two weeks," the woman said impassively as she carried the now-silent child away toward the food court. Mara wondered what kind of mother the child would have once she returned. If she returned.

A crust punk who was mostly earlobes stood in line

for the Roulette box, which resembled a mall photo booth. When the door slid open, Mara could see the globe-shaped structure inside illuminated by the pacific glow of the betting screen. On this screen, players placed bets corresponding to the granularity of the topological transformation they wished to undergo. The higher the bet, the smaller the unit of self the transformation applied to, the longer the time spent digitized, and the higher the cash payout afterward. Ultimately there was no way to accurately guess how each bet would interact with an individual's space-time tubeform. Some players had been in the system since its creation.

The door to the Roulette box slid open. The punk with the earlobes stomped toward it, glancing around for an audience like a child does before deciding to initiate a shriek. Mara glimpsed the spherical grid of specialized cameras that would digitize the player's three-dimensional form and upload it into the Casino's system, leaving the Roulette box empty for the next player. The scanned form underwent a series of transformations that sheared the now-incorporeal body into hundreds and thousands of iterations of noise and static, each occupying an adjacent coordinate in toroidal space-time. Eventually—there was no guarantee how long it might take—the bits returned to their original locations. The body was then restored and downloaded back into the reception box.

The neutral glow of the betting screen intensified as Earlobes entered the box. The door closed and locked with a sibilant compression, aquamarine light spilling from the hair-thin spaces around its edges. A female speech emulator's voice could be faintly heard through the walls of the box.

An individual's experience of life through time is a four-dimensional representation of a higher-order shape. The same way that an architect's representation of a building from the side obscures the details of the far side of the building, so does the experience of life and the process of identity-formation obscure the full shape of who we could be. What lies on the other side of our thoughts, emotions, and decisions? When viewed from a "top-down" angle, the full plan can be seen at once. For the first time in history, the Casino is proud to offer the opportunity to experience the vastness that is you.

As if on cue, cornflower-colored pain sparkled down Mara's limbs through the fuses of her nerves, causing her to make a sound with her tongue and touch her temple in a pointless motion. Plucking a pill from her bag, she headed toward the exit and steeled herself against the excruciating number of minutes it would take for her stomach acids to release the analgesic compounds. Mara activated protective thoughts.

She reached first for her favorite memory: the first time that she saw Arlo and felt confronted by his incandescence. He was quiet, but something from the inside of him surged outward. She would later conceptualize it as rage. His eyelids lifted just enough to take in what was right in front of him, and she found this motion to be lovely, even erotic, coupled with the black pinpoints contracting and expanding in fields of hazel.

Mara walked quickly out of the Casino, reaching further into the banks of her memory. Arlo's face turned into that of her high school boyfriend, who'd been pale and thin and had a face rosy with acne that gave his form a kind of blushing quietness. His acne had never bothered Mara; she'd never even seen it as something separate from the texture of his skin—pleasingly rough like homemade paper. He used to smile in bright flashes that were followed by a sudden vulnerability. He would close his lips tightly then, seemingly determined not to let that kind of thing slip again.

And then there was a boy in Mara's middle school whose face rippled in a strange way, his blond hair and tan skin all the same shade and blending into each other like sand dunes, studded with eyes like sea glass. Having emigrated from Mexico, he spoke halting English in the dented, smoky voice of adolescence. On the first day of high school, she saw him, taurus-like and enormous. He had injected steroids so that he could be a linebacker. Though of course it was still technically visible, his face had somehow disappeared.

Mara tried to hold onto the memory of these faces as her painkillers kicked in and her brisk pace slowed to a trudge. A dissociative side effect seemed to scramble her understanding of where her limbs were in space. Her knees and elbows felt indistinguishable. The interior of her body felt much larger than it appeared from the outside. She could see her building take shape up ahead, but it seemed to be getting farther away instead of closer. Finally, a cold doorknob materialized under her hand. She shuffled through a series of keys and doors as exhaustion overtook her entirely. During these times, she preferred to retreat under a blanket and shut out all visual stimuli as she applied sadness to her body like a cold cream, chilling and unctuous, a mysterious but necessary cleansing ritual before her consciousness converted pixel by pixel into sleep.

———

Arlo was picking through their mail at the kitchen table when Mara entered the apartment. He handed her a red cardboard box.

"This came for you," he said.

She thanked him and sliced the box open with a paring knife. Packed neatly inside were a small silver drive and several instructional pamphlets.

When she was young, Mara used to flip through the lifestyle magazines displayed at grocery store check-out lines and do the personality tests at the end of each section.

What kind of perfume would you wear on a hot date?
    A.   Something floral and feminine
    B.   Something fresh and clean
    C.   Something exotic and spicy
    D.   Nothing, I like my natural scent

She would keep track of her answers in her mind by making them into a mnemonic. ABDDBA. All big dummies don't buy art. She was always disappointed by the results of the tests.

Your perfect wedding colors are bright and bold, just like you!

She always hoped that instead it would say something to the effect of: *Your perfect wedding color is slate. Just slate, and nothing else. Think about a wedding that is a sea of slate, with no flowers, no sparkling lights, nothing but sheet rock for decoration. That is probably something you would find lovely.*

Holding the drive and the instructional pamphlets in her hand had sparked this memory, which Mara noticed but released quickly like one would something wriggling.

———

Arlo watched Mara open the red box. Her face had begun to take on the quality of lamé. It shone and appeared liquid at times, as if a bug landing on her cheek might send ripples into her mouth. At other times, the lines of her face hardened into sharp metallic edges. She always seemed to be trembling.

Mara turned to leave the kitchen.

"What is it?" Arlo asked her.

"My results."

Resisting the urge to follow her into the room, Arlo went back to looking through the mail. Their conflicts had shifted from small perceptions of disrespect to questioning what things had happened and how much they could be said to have happened. Mara was losing her memory, that much was clear. Her day-to-day actions had taken on a Markovian quality in which the past was as informationless as the future. Cooking an egg did not need to be done the way it had always been done; the process could be reinvented each day. One time at a party he had to stop her from disrobing entirely because she was curious to see what would happen. To Arlo, Mara had become a scribble devoid of logic, whose persistence in existing anyway was at once marvelous and terrifying. When he held her while they slept, he felt as if their bodies were being warmed by the heat of the extinguishing pieces of her memory.

———

When she first returned from the Roulette system, Mara was a human-shaped rubber band ball. Her knees were the gray of old elastics and supported her weight about as well. When Arlo tried to embrace her, she ricocheted off his chest. When she spoke, her words were no longer delivered in a California drawl; they had an unplaceable yet strangely familiar inflection.

For several weeks afterward, Mara had tried to self-soothe by reading books but found herself fixated on the object of the book itself, perceiving it not as a unitary entity but instead as a *process* of tiny particles clinging to each other through electrochemical forces. All objects seemed to be imbued with an alien sense of temporality. Symbols that she had been able to read with ease and fluency in the past now seemed to explode with meaning, each letter of the alphabet vomiting up a multitude of semantic content. Every possible nuance of the letter "s" was communicated in one viewing. Reading quickly became torturous.

Light switch plates on the walls beckoned her with implications. Why was it placed at that level on the wall? What was behind it? Why was the plastic that particular shade of beige? The first time Mara had entered her bedroom after playing Roulette, she'd felt as if she were walking into a wax museum. All her things looked like cheaply constructed reproductions that had been moved from their usual locations, though nothing was actually out of place.

Mara entered the bedroom holding the red box at her breast like a wounded bird. She flipped the light switch and flooded the bedroom with bright orange. Noting the continued presence of *jamais vu*, Mara sat on the bed and opened the red box.

The following is a guide to help you interpret the results of your recent GUA test.

> *1.   Connect the drive to a laptop with three-dimensional display capability.*
> *2.   Open the folder labeled **Results** with any standard three-dimensional imaging software.*
> *3.   You will see a hemicube with three axes labeled **Activation**, **Information Source**, and **Modulation**.*
> *4.   Clicking **Modulation** will open a second hemicube in a new window with three axes labeled **Norepinephrine**, **Serotonin**, and **Acetylcholine**.*

The shape of the data points within each window reflects aspects of your affective functioning. Data points clustered at various sections in the first cube represent different consciousness states. In Diagram 1 these areas are represented as follows:

A.   *Standard waking state*

B.   *NREM sleep*

C.   *REM sleep*

Under normal physiological conditions, an individual's cluster of data points cycles between these three areas throughout a twenty-four-hour period. Our research has shown that Ruga individuals experience a different cycle from the general population, inhabiting unusual areas of the cube throughout the day. Some individuals do not seem to cycle at all—these types of distributions are correlated with hyperlability in mood and more severe difficulties with memory consolidation. See Diagrams 2–6 for examples.

The results of your test will be used to map your microexpressions to neurotransmitter activity as well as consciousness phase states. Our goal is to use the information from this mapping to develop a codex that will improve communication between Ruga and non-Ruga individuals.

You have an upcoming appointment with your neurologist at the Casino to discuss your results. Please bring a written list of questions or concerns you would like addressed. The next step will involve coming to the GUA Lab for a sleep study monitoring your PGO waves. We at the GUA Lab thank you for your service.

"Can you read these instructions to me?" Mara leaned in the kitchen doorway, her face drawn. Arlo looked up from chopping an onion, tears streaming down his face. Mara stared at the linoleum floor. "I'm having a hard time understanding."

———

The surgery was Arlo's idea. Mara had woken up shivering at six o'clock one morning—some two weeks after she'd rematerialized in the Roulette box—apparently with the intention of taking apart a light switch plate with a screwdriver. From bed, Arlo saw her digging through his toolbox. He tried weakly to dissuade her.

"Baby," he called.

She was wearing three of his sweaters but had not put on pants, which made her look like an overgrown child. She did not answer him but instead furiously screwed and unscrewed the same screw.

"What are you doing?" he tried again.

She ignored him, yelling, "What?" several minutes later. Arlo had already drifted back to sleep. He returned from work that evening with candles for the room.

"I need an outlet," she cried as he walked through the front door. She had put on a fourth sweater and was sweating and shivering with electronics scattered around her.

"There's an outlet right there." Arlo pointed in bewilderment to an electrical outlet on the wall, though he saw upon closer inspection that its entrails had been removed.

"No!" Tears were streaming down Mara's face. "Don't make fun of me."

"What? I'm not!" Arlo wondered whether he should call a doctor. "Are you feeling all right?" He went over to her and tried to take off a sweater.

"I need an outlet," Mara sobbed with her arms up. "I'm experiencing a lot of things and it's building up inside of me." Arlo wrestled one sweater off.

"You know you can always talk to me. Why are you wearing so many sweaters and no pants?"

"I'm cold but also hot. Talking makes it worse. I feel stupid, like I'm being trampled by something in slow motion."

Arlo peeled each sweater off Mara's body and wrapped her in a blanket. She stopped crying and immediately fell asleep in his arms.

When she awoke over fourteen hours later, Arlo

brought her a bowl of microwaved soup and sheets of printouts, which he read aloud, about the way Ruga surgery allowed people to return to a relatively normal life after going into the Roulette system. The procedure was still considered to be experimental and was therefore free for anyone who wanted it.

His well-intentioned suggestion that she surgically alter her face produced an internal storm so disproportionately painful for Mara that she agreed to it the very next day. Arlo called the Casino and made an appointment for her. If all went well, he expected that the surgery would be an imperfect but acceptable conclusion to the worst event of their life.

———

The surgery was over quickly, with minimal bruising. Mara could hardly tell that it had happened at all except that she no longer felt like a stretched slingshot. She was able to plan her days again and apply for jobs. She could read again, albeit very slowly. She could even write a little bit.

Unfortunately and despite expectations to the contrary, Mara's episodes of frantic curiosity only seemed to intensify after the surgery. Mysterious triggers compelled her to search for patterns. She started keeping a spreadsheet of small actions she did throughout the day.

> *Breakfast leftover cheese*
> *Cried in shower*
> *Out of coffee no coffee today*
> *Arlo said something I couldn't hear, didn't ask to repeat, afraid might be I love you*
> *Lunch Pop-Tarts*
> *Felt antsy for most day*

But writing took enormous effort, and she found the spreadsheet to be too linear. So Mara began to draw mandalas of connectomes between actions, events, and reflections. When Arlo insisted that it was her turn to do the laundry because it was an odd-numbered month, Mara felt a familiar coldness come over her. Why did she have a distinct memory of turning on a washing machine last month? Her mandala showed her that she had offered to do the laundry out of turn that month because she felt guilty about ruining Arlo's life. Relief swept over her at the sight of the memory and she happily lugged the mesh bag of clothes to the laundromat.

Soon the mandalas grew into the air for lack of floor

space in the closet. Mara constructed them from wire and brown wrapping paper. She developed a series of markings in white paint that symbolized people, qualifiers, and relationships. Nodes and branches of the mandala tree multiplied and events became more fine-grained, taking on the appearance of a swarm of insects frozen into mesh. Mara tended to it with an understanding that once the topiary revealed to her the final pattern of her illness, she would be able to show it to Arlo, who would finally understand.

Arlo, for his part, had stopped trying to understand. At first, he had tried to ask Mara about what happened to her in the Roulette box. But her inability to tell him frustrated him so much that he eventually stopped asking. The intensity with which they used to communicate through glances was gone. Mara's new gaze was often fixed on the floor. He thought about his own parents, who at this point only communicated by screaming at each other. Arlo knew his parents well enough to understand that the screams expressed not anger but an acknowledgment that the unstoppable cold drift of time between them could not be bridged, and that they would soon be reduced to shouting simple instructions to each other from distant ice floes until their deaths.

The decision not to tell anyone about Mara's condition was not made consciously. When his boss pointed out that he'd been spending less time in the lab, Arlo fabricated an illness for himself to avoid questions he didn't have answers to. Thankfully, a scientist from Belgium had just joined the lab for a semester and was now occupying most of his boss's attention. The visiting researcher, Hanne, had silver hair—a healthy sheet of platinum blonde cropped near her ears. Her bright pink cheeks emanated productive vitality. Several times a day, Arlo found his attention drifting from his bench toward Hanne and the way her hair lit up like LED fibers in the sunlight while she sliced frozen mouse brains at the cryostat. The objective lens on the microtome produced a high-resolution, brilliantly colorized picture of each section of the brain as she rotated the handwheel with both care and nonchalance, like a metaphysical butcher processing some priceless deli meat.

Mara had spent three weeks in the official Casino Roulette system, a fairly average length of time. She was one of the luckier ones. There were secret basement clubs across the world that allowed people to experience an unofficial version of the system. They all used the same cheap algorithm and were far more dangerous than the Casino's. Many people reassembled back into their seats from digitization lifeless and cold: skin mottled, eyes frozen in animal panic, limbs in unexpected orientations. Police would sometimes sweep as many as a dozen bodies from a single basement.

Arlo had just rolled and smoked a joint when he received a phone call from the Casino informing him that someone entering the Roulette system had given his number as an emergency contact.

"Why?" he had asked.

"Excuse me?"

"Did she give a reason as to why she did it?"

The voice on the other end laughed and hung up.

Arlo camped out in front of the screens for hours after work each night, eating buttered rice from a Tupperware container and trying to catch a glimpse of Mara's form in the grid of screens filled with static. Several times he thought that he recognized her collarbones in the noise. His mother called him every day during those weeks, advising him to move on with his life or at least join a support group. He did neither. Arlo spent those three weeks in a state of suspended animation, doing the bare minimum to get by. It was as if his brain had turned off unnecessary networks and was using its energy reserves for the sole act of visual scanning.

Paradoxically, the most intense sensation for Mara immediately following the spherical grid of camera flashes was that of her body ceasing to exist. Her vestibular structures still appeared to be functioning, for she felt a tug at her belly button and a rush of forward motion, but Mara could no longer tell whether her eyes were open or closed, whether she was breathing or not breathing, whether her tongue was still in her mouth or lolling between parted lips, or any of the other things human beings are supposed to be aware of regarding their bodies.

After returning from the system, Mara did not understand the meaning of words. A piece of metal with the words RADIANT HEAT MANIFOLD stopped her dead in her tracks. She looked at it for several minutes inside of a train station, her body a motionless island in eddies of hurrying people. Interpretations of each word spun and synchronized like reels in a slot machine.

After returning from the system, each morning Mara forgot who she had been the day before. Every day showed her a new world. On some days the warm glow of recognition would saturate her as Arlo walked through the door, after which she'd smile and tell him to come here. On other days, it would be as if a stranger had walked in. The unfamiliar lines of his body filled her with anxiety salted with desire. It was Mara's perpetual astonishment at Arlo's beauty that propelled her forward from day to day, like a quick shove into a cold pool. If she could climb out of it, then the rest of the day would go easily. The anxiety took hold when she observed that nothing in Arlo's motions toward her indicated that he felt anything like desire at this point in their relationship or, even more frighteningly, that he had ever felt it at all.

After returning from the system, Mara no longer remembered that while in the system she had experienced millions of lifetimes, with hundreds of millions of years passing by in full detail. If she had, she might have died from the sheer enormity of such a memory. Instead, the memory had been compressed into a rather inconvenient syndrome, a voice that continually whispered *don't forget, don't forget, you already know everything you will ever need to know.*

Mara was in a large room with a black-and-white checkered floor that held a tangible manifestation of sound. The sound was that of an explosion.

She awoke with a start. Her sheets were soaked, and her first thought was that she had wet herself. She looked down at her body and realized it was sweat. Pushing the covers away in a Herculean effort, Mara touched a toe to the cold floor. Shivering, she peeled off her wet T-shirt and pulled on an orange nylon jacket.

Short fever dreams were the only ones that Mara had anymore. She had them frequently. Her doctor said that this was a good thing because it meant she hadn't yet lost the protective ability to undergo REM sleep.

In the kitchen, Mara cracked an egg straight into her mouth and swallowed it. She then cracked open a beer and drank the whole thing, along with three pills to keep her fever down. Her long black hair had turned completely silver and she had lost thirty pounds, giving her otherwise youthful face a premature gauntness. The boutique had fired her the week before—partly for rearranging the store without permission, but mostly for making the customers uncomfortable.

"This is a store where people should not be scared to

bring their children," her boss had explained.

Since then, Mara had been spending her days watching the screens at the Casino or napping fitfully. Today, however, she was headed somewhere else.

It was two in the afternoon when Mara walked into a dark bar filled with people. There were muffled conversations here and there, the sound of glasses being picked up and put down, the heavy clacks of pool balls scattering. A black-and-red velvet painting of a panther loomed on one wall. Mara sat down at an empty table and looked around. The two people at the table next to her were looking at each other, the contours of their faces constantly shifting and rearranging like text in a dream. Mara looked farther down. Groups of people were gathered, sitting silently, not speaking but seemingly communicating. There were bursts of laughter and sips of beer.

An older man shaped like a mountain was playing chess against himself. He looked over at Mara and smiled not with his mouth but solely with his cheeks, which ruffled like the downy feathers of a dove. Mara was suddenly struck by the unambiguous sense of recognition. She wondered which part of her deleted life he might have belonged to.

"I like that jacket," the chess player said.

"Thank you." Mara hesitated. "This may sound strange, but have we met before?"

"I don't believe so. I'm George," he said, and extended his hand.

"Mara."

The chessboard George was playing on was not a grid; instead, it resembled magnified lace. As Mara watched this new form of gameplay in which the pieces moved in curves and spirals, she smiled too.

Abstract:

The explosion of research conducted on the nature of the Ruga experience has given the scientific community much to consider about the future of human communication. The deterioration of verbal communication between Ruga and non-Ruga individuals provides strong evidence for the modality-as-membrane hypothesis. This hypothesis states that certain modes of subjective experience contain strange attractors that socially bifurcate populations through nontrivial ontological processes. In the case of the Ruga, a unique modality of information transference acts as a social-ecological barrier. Genetic drift has not yet been observed but should be monitored for.

The novel nature of communication dynamics in Ruga

populations opens up an immense new field of study. One promising avenue of inquiry, upon a review of existing literature, is the possibility of self-selection based on differential biomass allocations in the fusiform gyrus (the facial recognition apparatus of the brain) due to ontogenetic drift. Our recommendations involve further funding in both quantitative and phenomenological research in the target population.

Research reported in this review was supported by GUA Institute, the Casino, and the National Institute of Neurological Disorders and Stroke of the National Institutes of Health under award number Q9658939.

George slid the study toward his new boss, Derek Westing, Jr., over a complicated mirrored surface meant to emulate a speculative process not achievable in human time frames or at human processing speeds. The table had belonged to the late Dr. Westing, George's old boss, who by the time of his death George had come to think of as a father.

"I think there's something here," he said, pointing to a line he had highlighted in yellow-green: *Our recommendations involve further funding in both quantitative and phenomenological research in the target population.* "Each year there are fewer and fewer grants in the sciences. Labs fight over them like dogs. Each year there are more and more grants in the humanities that languish before they're rerouted to the sciences to be fought over. Why not cut out the extra step and take an anthropological approach to our problem? Or a philosophical one? Or whichever one we can secure funding for?"

George's boss, a man both younger and less experienced than he was, looked down at the reflective surface of the table with a thumbnail inserted between his teeth. He said nothing for a long time.

"Listen," he said finally. "I appreciate this idea, and in general what you're trying to do here. But we simply don't have the resources to pivot like this. We can't just hire all new staff researchers to devote to solving a problem that—to be honest—isn't all that interesting or promising, market-wise. We've tried the Ruminous project before, remember? It failed, and quite catastrophically. There's no point in beating that dead horse."

"I know, I was the lead developer. It's different this time. We've had many discussions about how exactly it's different this time," George said as calmly as he could. "Our past failures pave the way for our future successes, as your father liked to say," he added. "He understood what the Ruminous project had the power to become."

Westing Jr. sighed. He looked at George's reflection in the statistically determined laminate pattern of the tabletop. The palindromic angle of his mouth betrayed nothing except a mild contempt. "Go ahead and put together a dossier for me containing every single report we might possibly use to apply for these grants. Tell Jordan to put out an ad for one—just ONE—anthropology intern from the university. We'll meet again in a couple months before deadlines and figure out how to move forward."

———

It had rained all night after several days of clear skies. Chanterelles were fruiting in flaming bundles under oak trees. Five friends piled into Arlo's silver sedan in a tumble of wool caps and windbreakers. While the others went stomping into the woods for mushrooms, Mara and Paula stayed behind to collect wildflowers. They gathered golden poppies, violet larkspurs, daisies, mariposa lilies, starflowers, and dry fairy lanterns. Mara felt peaceful being there with the flowers and Paula, a person who rarely drew attention to herself and seemed to float through life with the gentle pulse of a jellyfish. Mara felt envious of this quality, as her own hypervisibility made her feel deeply obnoxious just for existing. She wished desperately to learn how to live the rest of her life as a ghost.

Mara fingered a long stem with bright glossy leaves and a cluster of red flowers. A plant's body is nothing but a map of its decisions, the extruded structures of excess energy. In its youth this plant had manically made leaves out of hunger. Once the green tongues had lapped up enough sunlight, the plant had some time to think about its future and what kinds of things it might like. Being fixed to the ground, the plant wanted to be able to make love to itself. An inflorescence occurred. The plant grew rudimentary organs to be able to say its own name. When that wasn't enough, the plant wanted to make love to others. It developed crimson petals that helped it to transport its love through the draw of beauty. The charm worked as well on bees as it did on humans, and what was once a modest desire for love was bred into the inflated cartoons of sex parts used in bundles during human courtship rituals. In this way, the plant sees the world.

Mara picked one of the red flowers and handed it to Paula, who threaded it into her crown. Paula wore it at the dinner table as she heaped mushroom risotto onto everyone's plate. Unlike people, who must sometimes supplement their lack of physical charm with works of great beauty and taste, a plant's life's work is its phenotype. In the subconscious annals of Mara's memory lay dormant the knowledge that this was the form she had seen in the system: her own gasping, pulsating shape over time, a globular tube of automatic behaviors punctuated by nodes of decisions glowing like endlessly reflective jewels.

———

Arlo left his car in the empty parking lot of the laboratory and ascended the after-hours stairs into the rodent holding room. The holding room was lit by a dim red light, which made it resemble the inside of a lung. Arlo pulled one of the mice from its cage and weighed it. He then put it back in its cage and wheeled it into the dissection room, where he placed it into a clear acrylic case the size of a music box with two tubes. The isoflurane tanks were empty now due to budget cuts. Arlo turned the CO_2 pump on low. At first, the mouse sniffed curiously at the corners of the box. As the gas released, the animal's motions slowed until it passed out, its tiny lungs working under delicate ribs. Arlo cranked the pump and left the silky grey shape to slowly asphyxiate while he set up the guillotine.

Some of the mice he worked on that night didn't pass out so peacefully. They struggled to escape and clawed at the walls of the case, releasing a panic pheromone that steadily accumulated in the chamber and could not be wiped away. Since all the mice in one cohort had to be sacrificed on the same day, there wasn't much that could be done. By the time Arlo opened the lid to sacrifice the last mouse several hours later, the box was overflowing with the scent of horror.

The last mouse's frightened scratching slowed as it crumpled, disoriented, in a corner. Arlo watched the clock impatiently. Though Mara's retrograde amnesia showed no signs of dissipating, she was slowly getting better and was able to form new memories more or less normally. But he still didn't like leaving her alone for such long periods of time at night. Often he wondered what Mara's life would have been like if she hadn't dropped out of graduate school to move across the country with him for this job. Maybe she would've had a better career, more friends, or something else that would've kept her from playing Roulette. He wondered what his own life would have been like without her.

This now-familiar pattern of wondering always ended in the guilty contemplation of whether it was his research that gave Mara the idea to play Roulette. He recalled the vaguely annoying manner in which her eyes always seemed to glaze over when he tried to explain the minutiae of his work to her. He had always assumed that she was not paying attention.

The dark clouds outside meant rain. Arlo was tired of rain. He took the final mouse out of the box and made a small incision near its sternum, where he planned to insert a needle in order to pump out the blood and perfuse the little body with saline and paraformaldehyde. Arlo reached over the pump to grab a new needle, but when he turned back, the mouse was gone. He groaned deeply as he watched a grey shape dash under a bench. He had forgotten to crank the CO_2.

Arlo searched for the mouse for twenty minutes or so before giving up. Little specks of blood here and there on the floor failed to lead him to the animal. He left a note for the janitorial service and recorded the loss of a homozygous PrP specimen in his notebook. Each sick or lost animal also meant the loss of months and thousands of dollars' worth of work. It was embarrassing and frustrating when things like this happened, and it seemed to Arlo that they were happening more frequently.

———

"Did the janitors ever find the mouse?"

Arlo opened his eyes to see Hanne leaning over him, smiling. He instinctively touched his mouth to make sure he hadn't been drooling in his sleep. He had been, a little. Arlo sat up in his chair and looked around. The lab was deserted. Hanne was glowing like a specter in her lab coat, so close he could identify the kind of beer she had drunk earlier that night on her breath. It was an unfiltered wheat. He cleared his throat and tried to speak but nothing came out.

"No," he finally said. "No sign of it."

"That's spooky, no? I keep thinking that I will accidentally find it under my shoe." She showed him the soles of her black leather flats.

"It is a little strange, I guess," Arlo said, trying to slide his chair away from Hanne without her noticing. "They're so small though. I imagine it ran out without anyone seeing."

Hanne tucked her hair behind her ear, showing an imperfect pearl embedded in her earlobe.

"Or maybe it died somewhere. It did have a hole

in its chest," Arlo continued. His heart was pounding loudly. Hanne peered at his chest, as if she could hear it. She laughed in a way that both hurt and felt good.

"You are funny," she said.

"Thanks," he said awkwardly. The lab seemed more humid than normal. Hanne was still looking at him. Arlo shifted in his chair.

"What time is it? I'm funnier in the morning. I should probably go home."

"Yes, it is late," Hanne said, and looked away. "I think past midnight."

"Do you need a ride home?" Arlo asked, knowing it was the correct thing to say but hoping the increasingly obvious fact that he was terrified of her would prompt Hanne to decline.

"No, thanks," she said. "I still have some things to finish up here." She moved toward the walk-in cold storage. "Has anyone ever been trapped in this room that you know of?" she asked over her shoulder as she shook a container of nasal spray.

"Not that I know of," he responded, swaying on his feet. He had stood up from his chair too quickly and was swatting at a swarm of phosphenes about his head.

"Check for my body in the morning," Hanne said, smiling. "Good night."

She disappeared into the freezer.

On the drive home, Arlo turned off the music in his car, which was unusual for him. He believed that when he was tired, a rhythmic propulsion helped him drive better. But tonight, he was more interested in replaying the conversation with Hanne in his head over and over again.

It felt good to be visible to a woman again, though the scrutinizing force of Hanne's golden eyes felt unexpectedly extreme, as if a stage light had blasted him in the face without warning. He wondered whether Hanne might have caught him staring at her over the last several weeks. He did not like the possibility that his private thoughts might be communicated mutinously by his body.

Though he did not admit it to himself, Arlo had spent his life cultivating a preference for plain, smart women. He did not enjoy sensory assaults. The rather average geometric distributions of Mara's form were not what had drawn him to her. Her affectionate nature, lively speech, and general spontaneity were comforts he could sink into. The rare moments of weakness in which he desired beautiful women made his life feel disordered and foreign.

At a red light, Arlo considered taking a U-turn back to the lab and seeing if Hanne was still around. Suddenly disturbed by the direction his thoughts were taking, he turned the radio on.

The Casino has been a pioneer in the High-Risk, High-Reward research movement over the last decade. The astonishing number of biomedical devices produced by researchers at the Casino has once again pushed the United States to the forefront of the international research community.

In developing a model of science funding that relies on subject pay-in, the institute has seen a steady flow of funding for basic, translational, and clinical grants examining new developments in all areas of health and medicine.

This model has also diversified subjects from the WEIRD model—western, educated, and from industrialized, rich, and democratic countries. A significant portion of subjects in the new model are low-income immigrants with little to no formal education. Though issues of population self-selection continue to confound results, self-reporting and genetic testing has shown an overall increase in

diversity of genes, attitudes, and behavior in recruited sub-
jects. The model has also provided a productive alternative
to welfare for the unemployed, acting as a source of income
as well as entertainment.

In this hour, we talk to various individuals—scientists,
ethicists, and someone who has been asleep for a very long
time—about the Casino's contributions to science, as well
as the implications of what are possibly the most important
advances in psychiatric medicine of this century. I'm Peter
Sokolov, your host for the hour.

A hopeful score played under the host's tidy sen-
tences.

Peter: *The topic of discussion for today: egos and cas-*
kets. Well, EGO and E-CASC, to be precise. Externally
Generated Object Therapy, or EGO The, took the decep-
tively simple concept behind mirror therapy for phantom
limb pain and applied it through a fascinating new image
production technology to produce a treatment for body dys-
morphia with an 80 percent success rate. Just to be clear,
rates like this are unheard of. Or rather, they used to be.

EGO was later adapted into the infamous Roulette sys-
tem that, along with another Casino-developed invention
called E-CASC, has virtually eliminated suicide in the

Western hemisphere. We'll tackle EGO in the second half of the show. For now, I'm here with Dr. Sun Shang, one of the original creators of E-CASC, to learn more. Welcome to the show, Dr. Shang.

Sun: *Thank you, Peter. It's great to be here. And please, call me Sun.*

Peter: *So what is E-CASC? How would you explain it to someone who has never heard of it?*

Sun: *E-CASC stands for Emergency Consciousness/ Alertness System Cessation. I like to think of it as "sleep mode." Essentially, it allows people who are in a lot of pain or are very tired to take some time off from the incessant demands of everyday life without resorting to suicide. Most people are more familiar with Roulette, so I'll use it as a point of reference. If Roulette lets you hit the restart button on your brain, E-CASC lets you hit pause. You're still the exact same person, just very well rested.*

Peter: *Fascinating. How does it work? I'm imagining Han Solo being frozen in carbonite.*

Sun: *[Laughing] You can think of it that way, but it's not so cold and static. People who are in E-CASC are basically in a state of induced coma. We have them placed in a specialized holding cell with machines that help them breathe, help their fluids pump, rotate their body this way and that so they don't get bedsores—basically everything they'll need* *to survive intact until the next Rouse/Arousal Day. Oh, and we replace their blood with liquid glass.*

Peter [voiceover]: *Wow, a lot to unpack there. I really wanted to know more about the liquid glass, but we had a lot of material to cover and not a lot of time. So I charged forward. Sun, what on earth is Rouse/Arousal Day?*

Sun: *Every three years or so, a cohort of individuals are "woken up," so to speak, and live out in the world for some time to decide whether they'd like to continue living outside E-CASC.*

Peter: *Wild! What does that look like?*

Sun: *Most people aren't even aware of it. We don't exactly publicize the day, or much else about our functions. But for us researchers, it's a bit like watching a swarm of locust nymphs suddenly burst from under the earth. These people, whom we've all gotten to know so intimately through their biodata, suddenly animate into living, breathing, and suffering human beings. And all in one day. We lead them out into the world, sometimes holding them by the elbow, and—well, let's just say the biblical metaphors write themselves.*

Peter: *Wow. Wild, wild stuff. By the way, what's with the odd naming convention with the slash? Rouse-slash-Arousal?*

Sun: *[Laughing] Well, Peter, it really speaks to the uncertainty of what we're working with. Ever since we created*

E-CASC there has been a philosophical divide about what's really going on. Are we turning the volume down just on alertness or on consciousness altogether? Are patients being roused from sleep, or are they being aroused or stimulated? Is there an appreciable difference? We simply don't know.

Peter [voiceover]: *So this got me thinking, naturally, about the Ruga. One of the biggest questions our country is grappling with right now is why exactly people play Roulette and enter into this radically new existence that, for all intents and purposes, is like choosing to go mad. What's their motivation? So I went to MIT to talk to Professor Gina Shertona, the creator of EGO, about the technology's most famous application: the Roulette system. Thanks so much for being on the show, Dr. Shertona.*

Dr. Shertona: *It's my pleasure, Peter.*

Arlo pulled into the driveway and turned the car off. All the lights in the house were on.

———

Mara had developed specific aversions and fears that bordered on the unreasonable. One of these was a fear of bags. Their darkness seemed to contain unknown fanged things that might bite her fingers as they rummaged.

"Could you throw me my cigarettes?" Arlo once asked her. "They're in my blue bag next to you."

"How do you know?" Mara asked him.

"What do you mean? That's where I left them," Arlo said.

"Yes, but how do you know that's where they are now? What if they're somewhere else and don't materialize in the bag until the moment I reach my hand in to grab them? Or even worse, what if they don't materialize at all, but something else does?"

Arlo rolled his eyes. "I think there's a high probability that my cigarettes have not been magically replaced by something else," he said as he walked over to his bag, noting a sudden and very real sense of dread as he reached into its toothed mouth.

Despite the odd elaborations, Arlo had hoped that the stabilizing effect of Ruga surgery, combined with the clothes hanging in her closet, her books on the bookshelf, the photos of herself among friends on the refrigerator, and the other aspects of their collected life together would jog Mara toward herself. But she looked at the detritus of her past self the way a child looks at a textbook: dispassionately, and only when quizzed.

Sometimes Arlo's stomach would do a backflip

when he'd come home to see Mara sitting by the record player, framed by the lavender sky and pink clouds outside the window, listening to the same *tarana* over and over again. Would she remember the way she used to dance, white silk skirt flaring out from her waist like a morning glory unfurling, black hair coming undone from the braid pinned to her waist by a large wool belt? And indeed there was a searching look in her eyes while she listened, like Radha looking for Krishna.

But as soon as the *tarana* ended, Mara turned back into a person without a name.

———

"How does it work?" Arlo had asked once as they lay stretched out on their bed, luxuriating in the heat of an unseasonably sunny Saturday. This was several months after Mara's surgery, which had removed the painful pressure that would otherwise build up behind her eyes during any form of physical intimacy. "How do you talk without words?"

"The same way it works when we fuck," Mara had said. "How do you know what I mean when I touch you where you want to be touched? It's the same thing." Mara's body had become so thin that her heart was visible under her skin, beating with the desperation of a slitted mouse.

"But you don't touch each other," Arlo protested.

No one ever touches anything. It's always just electrons interacting at surfaces that make it appear as if our tissues have bridged the gap between us and other things. But there is always a space, and we have begun to feel from afar, Mara wanted to say but didn't have the words. Instead her face became peachish and blurry, and she shrugged.

"We do, sort of," she said, and snuggled in toward Arlo's torso in a motion of sleep.

Arlo pressed on. "Why can't you translate what you're saying with your face into words? So I can understand."

Because how do you describe the color of a room with words? Sometimes a room is red or white because someone has made it that way. But most rooms are not a color that exists, they're the relationship of areas of light. If you try to trap such descriptions in containers of syntax, you'll only get the big, clumpy, ugly parts. But those descriptions can play on a face the way a fish gambols on water, a bluish fin breaking through here and there, making a slapping sound.

Mara felt this explanation inside of her but was unable to say it. In any case, she wasn't sure it would clarify anything.

Instead she said, "I really am sorry, I wish I could," and turned around to go to sleep.

———

Mara ripped off a corner of the pastry that she had just taken out of the oven and stuffed it into her mouth. The flaky crust crunched between her teeth while pockets of butter burst in hot blooms. She was Godzilla eating a city, savoring the wealthy neighborhoods. The doorbell rang.

George stood at the front door with a backpack slung over his shoulder. He wore a white polo shirt and dark jeans spackled with mud near the hem. Covered in grey stubble, his cheeks swirled like marble. Mara smiled back and gestured for him to come upstairs.

George sat on the couch and Mara sat on a green vinyl chair angled toward him. They looked at each other's faces as if they were screens. George seemed apprehensive. His gaze never left Mara's face, but his eyelids danced around the orbital cavities like dervishes. His dark skin contained whorls of lavender and light pink and green, as if the veins and capillaries under it were rearranging themselves into a more pleasing conformation. Mara felt flushed. They sat like this for a minute.

"Chess?" George asked eventually.

Mara shook her head no. George saw Mara's face radiate intense focus as she looked at him, her bones seeming to become dagger-like. Knowing that she had a boyfriend, he interpreted this focus in the way that would cause him the least amount of pain: she was at the vocabulary-acquiring stage of learning a new language.

As this interpretation occurred, George's eyelids danced slower. Mara immediately felt a sheer fabric drop between them and looked away. Arlo had left his work bag tipped over near the foot of the bed. George and Mara simultaneously noticed the form of a small gray mouse half-hidden under the bag's canvas flap. George walked over and carefully took the mouse out. He placed the stiff body on the table and pulled a plastic bag from his own backpack. From this he removed a bruised apricot, which he placed next to the mouse, and then a chanterelle mushroom, which he placed next to the apricot.

Mara looked at the table and suddenly understood. People always talk about the importance of knowing who you are and writing your life story. But her life did not seem to her like a story. It seemed more to her like this dead mouse, a deteriorating fruit, and a mushroom lined up in a row. As she looked at the three things on the table, she observed herself trying to extract meaning from them through various themes—nature, death, the branches of a phylogenetic tree. But she also considered concurrently that George's decision to arrange these objects on the table might not have any meaning whatsoever, and this thought was so remarkable to Mara that she consciously focused on it.

Purposeful meaninglessness. The more she focused on this, the more it produced a sensation of both fear and relief, which resulted in a burst of laughter that sprang from her lips in a sharp bark. Her mind raced. The idea that there might be agents in the world whose only goal was to slow the human race's suicidal sprint toward a pinprick of ultimate complexity by producing meaninglessness disguised as information became supremely comical, and Mara began to laugh even harder.

Or perhaps it was her? Had she finally come untethered from the remote control of signifiers? Was she finally free from the automatic tyranny of understanding? But no, that could not be it, since she had the distinct feeling of understanding, of experiencing insight, right at this very moment. This must have always been the human project: to get to a point in technological history when three things that could reasonably be seen, if nothing else, as disease vectors, or even food if you were really hungry—both rather compelling meanings for the majority of existence—could now be supplanted instead with the meaning content: null.

George laughed alongside Mara, though he had not meant to be funny.

"This is great," said Mara. "I feel like I get what's going on for the first time in a really long time. Thanks for coming over. Do you want a beer?"

Maury: *Sonia is furious with Dana because Dana left her to travel the cosmos and came back A FREAK!*

[Audience boos and hisses]

Maury: *Sonia, is there anything you'd like to say to Dana?*

Sonia: *Why did you do it? Why did you leave me?*

Dana: *[incomprehensible facial morphing]*

Sonia: *[crying] You lied to me, you lied, you lied, you lied, you lied to me. Now you won't even talk to me.*

Dana: *I'm trying &&&&&&&&&&&&&&&&&&&& Sonia &&&&&&&&&&&&&&&&&&*

Sonia's mother: *I told ya, these kinds of things don't work out. How you gonna love someone if you can't even talk to 'em?*

Dana's mother: *My daughter . . . MY DAUGHTER! My daughter doesn't need to be around people like you. I'm glad she found a girl like her! People like, like us . . . we can't love people like her without fetishizing them, and that's the goddamn truth.*

[Audience boos; some people in the audience clap]

Sonia's sister: *Y'all are fuckin' stupid. There ain't nothin' that happened to Dana. She just got the surgery so she could lie. Think about it: has she ever gone missing for weeks or months on end? The Casino will cut up anyone that asks 'em to. All the doctors there are full of shit. Just like Dana.*

[Audience screams]

Maury: *And we've sent a test to discover exactly that. Is Dana actually Ruga? Or is her appearance just a lie? Has this question been asked before? Can the Ruga lie?*

Mara got up to go to the bathroom. "Can we change the channel?"

"Sure, sorry," Arlo said, and flipped the television off. He looked up the episode on his phone and downloaded it to watch later.

Scrolling through his phone, Arlo looked at pictures from a backpacking trip in the mountains with some friends after college. They'd hiked ten miles through ice pinked by iron with everything they needed strapped to their backs. As they gained elevation, the nature of their conversations changed. The higher they got, the more secrets were revealed. At the very top of the mountain when they were certain that they would not encounter any other humans, they threw secrets into the gorge along with a large glass bottle of whiskey that was now empty.

"I regret my education!" Arlo had yelled.

"I do not love my family!!!!!" screamed Joe.

"I am unhappy about being short and take it out on others!!!!!!!!!!!!!!!" shrieked Li.

Everybody had laughed uproariously after each confession, mostly at the understanding that certain facts were only true at the top of a mountain and would deactivate at sea level. Whatever mystical force was responsible for the membrane rupture between individuals that allowed intimacy to bubble through, Arlo wished it didn't feel so far away.

Maybe he should plan another trip with the boys soon. Arlo called Li. It went to voicemail. He called Joe, who said he was away on a business trip but that he would call Arlo when he got back. Arlo knew it wouldn't happen and tried to carry this knowledge lightly. He felt that if he dropped dead right then and there, it was uncertain whether in his eulogy he would be described as a person who had many friends.

After Mara went to bed, Arlo googled Hanne's name on his phone. Considering the amount of space she was beginning to take up in his mental landscape, he did not know very much about her. He scrolled slowly through the various papers that she had authored during her short academic career and clicked on one entitled "The Effects of Intranasal OAN on Male and Female Affect Processing."

Abstract:

The neurobiological underpinnings of the Ruga experience are only beginning to be studied. The complex interaction between facial affect and emotional processing is of particular interest to researchers who hope to find in this new model of interaction some insight into altered social behavior in rare forms of dementia. Augmented social behavior in the Ruga suggests a biochemical pathway transformation. Animal models have shown vasopressin and oxytocin to be powerful chemical mediators of social behaviors—however, administering these peptides directly has produced negative results. Here we show that intranasal administration of OAN (OxyArgiNic), a synthetic analog of vasopressin, suspended in a standard BBBB (Blood-Brain Barrier Breaching) solution causes a substantial increase in affect recognition among adult non-Ruga males, greatly increasing the quantity and intensity of affective processing for several hours. We also show that the effect of OAN on affect recognition is reversed in adult non-Ruga females, causing a temporary reduction in both quantity and intensity of affective processing. These results concur with animal research suggesting an essential role for OAN as a therapeutic compound for affective processing, and open the door for future nonsurgical treatment options for those suffering from affective dementias and Post-Roulette Syndrome.

Arlo's eyes skimmed the abstract a second time while his mind wandered elsewhere. He then did the dishes from dinner and sidled into bed next to Mara. Turned away from him in the dark room, Mara's previously soft body was now thin and brittle, and—unbeknownst to him amid the haze of his own preoccupations—silently wished to be kissed between the shoulder blades.

Hanne came into the lab on a Sunday afternoon to set up an experiment for the next day. All the lights were on, but she was the only one there. Hanne leafed through her lab notebook until she found the recipe for creating a sucrose solution. Though the boring task of making solution stocks was now automated, she genuinely had nothing better to do.

Pouring scoops of pure white sugar into the tared plastic weighing boat reminded Hanne of helping her father make almond cakes on Christmas Day. Her job was to weigh out various fine powders into little cups and hand them to him. The care she took in measurement distracted her from the growling in her belly. She refused to eat anything all day until the moment the cake came out of the oven, infusing the entire house with the scent of creamy aldehyde. As the cake contained the energy of her own labor, eating it gave her a feeling of efficiency as well as a strange stirring of auto-eroticism. When the cake did not turn out so well, her father always took responsibility for whatever error had caused it to be so. Then Hanne felt satisfied, knowing that she had done her part correctly.

A freezer somewhere began to hum loudly. Hanne removed some sugar from the tray with a small metal instrument.

Photographs of a young woman with long dark hair were tacked around Arlo's computer with pushpins. In one picture, Arlo and the woman sat on the floor of an empty apartment along with several other friends. There was a plate of cookies in front of them, toward which both of their hands were outstretched. In another picture, the woman was in bed writing on a laptop, squinting bemusedly into the camera that had appeared over her head.

Hanne felt overcome with hunger and clutched the counter as if the ground were giving way beneath her. The feeling intensified. She tried to steady herself but felt as if she might faint. She grabbed the measuring boat filled with exactly 35 g of sugar and emptied it directly into her mouth.

After that she took a break to eat a Hot Pocket and watch part of a television show on her phone in the empty break room. During a commercial break, a news alert popped up.

Belgium has proposed a bill banning Ruga individuals from being employed in governmental positions. The rationale of the bill hinges on the claim that facial expressions are important visual signals that humans use to ascertain the intentions and mental states of others. The new and largely unknown expressions that define the Ruga condition

have the capacity to disrupt government functions, leading
to a disordered state of affairs, the bill claims. Ruga activ-
ists have characterized the bill as offensive, discriminatory,
and part of a protracted campaign to formally ascribe Ruga
to second-class citizen status in Belgium.

Hanne closed the alert. The next commercial was for allergy medication. A man gave a woman some flowers and said, "Because you are beautiful." The woman made a face as if she were about to sneeze but relaxed into a smile at the last minute. The man smiled also, glad that his gift had not been quashed by a systemic overreaction.

Plants, including flowers, were unremarkable to Hanne. She was perplexed when a friend took great pleasure in pointing out the silvery grey of a sidewalk weed or the bright yellow, stippled petals of a blossom shivering in the wind, or when a former boyfriend remarked on the manic, frilled tendrils of an asparagus fern with awe.

Hanne considered awe a naive and precious feeling in addition to an unfamiliar one. The only thing that came close for her was orgasm. She respected the orgasm for the way it barreled through her body like a freight train only to disappear without a trace and pursued it responsibly once a day by watching internet pornography on mute. This daily ritual tended to ward off ruder, more lingering sensations.

Hanne's phone lit up with a text.

Are you in lab? It was Arlo.

Yes. What's up?

Just forgot to put my wells in the freezer before I left, would you mind?

No, I can do it

Thanks...actually, I wanted to ask you something else

Hanne stared at the text.

Yes?

Kinda complicated, would prefer discussing in person. Nvm, i'll be in lab in 15 mins

See you soon

After finishing the Hot Pocket, Hanne locked herself in a bathroom stall to masturbate. She constructed in her mind's eye a person who might bring her flowers—an amalgamation of her plant-loving ex and the Romeo of the allergy medication commercial. Dark curls, dark skin, dark eyes. She was careful not to fold Arlo into the chimera. As her arousal ratcheted upward toward a familiar godhead, she was surprised to feel a brief sensation of awe at the fearsome enormity of her own loneliness.

"We always want people to meet us where we're at."

Hanne jumped. She hadn't seen Arlo approach her bench. "Sorry?"

"I just mean that when people are behaving unusually, or in a way that we don't understand, we always try to get them to come back to us. Maybe we should go to them instead."

Hanne nodded uncertainly.

"My girlfriend is Ruga," Arlo said. "I've been trying to get her to come back to me for some time now."

"Ah." Hanne nodded with certainty this time. She tried to ignore the despair looming on the horizon.

Arlo noticed Hanne's cheeks flushing to the shade of a Gala apple. He smiled. Apples were from the family *rosaceae*. The globular pearl in Hanne's earlobe seemed to rearrange its molecules slightly. Arlo blinked, suddenly feeling very tired.

"I saw your paper on OAN's effect on affective processing," he said.

"You did?" Hanne was taken aback. "Where did you find it?"

"Well, I saw the abstract. The paper was behind a rather expensive paywall."

"Yes, well, it was a very small, privately funded project. Nothing particularly interesting."

"It interests me very much," Arlo said. "I didn't know you'd done Ruga research."

"I haven't, really," Hanne said. Her flush was taking on tones of plum—also in the family *rosaceae*, Arlo couldn't help noting.

"I'm sorry," Arlo said. "This may seem strange, but I was wondering if I could see the recipe? For the OAN solution?"

"For what purpose?" Hanne asked, then quickly added: "The solution is no longer on the market. They pulled it some time ago."

"It's proprietary?"

"Yes."

"But you do know how to make it?"

"Yes," Hanne admitted. She seemed to be deliberately avoiding Arlo's gaze.

"Is something the matter?"

Hanne scanned Arlo's face. He was rumpled, with incandescent eyes and brows knitted intensely. Invisible ropes twisted in high tension seemed to be radiating outward from his pupils.

"You want the recipe for the OAN solution because you think it will help you communicate with your girlfriend."

"Yes," said Arlo.

"It will not work," said Hanne.

"How do you know?"

"Because," she hesitated. The freezer stopped humming abruptly, plunging the room into a conspicuous silence. Hanne allowed her finger to brush against Arlo's as she turned toward her bench.

"Because I use it all the time," she said quietly. "And it does not work very well."

"You use it all the time? Do you also have a Ruga partner?"

Hanne glanced at Arlo through the curtain of her own hair as she fiddled with a pipette. He did not seem to remember that OAN's effects were sex-specific, and she did not feel like reminding him.

"Not exactly."

"I don't understand," Arlo said.

"It doesn't matter," Hanne said. She picked up a pen absentmindedly and clicked it. Arlo thought she was going to write something down, but she just continued clicking it on and off. "So you want to consume a discontinued, non–FDA-approved psychotropic drug in order to get closer to your girlfriend? That is quite romantic."

"Why was it discontinued?"

"It gives people very bad cramps," Hanne responded.

"Well you've been doing it for a while, and you seem fine."

"Do I?" Hanne said as she continued clicking the pen.

The question caught Arlo off guard. "I understand it's a strange and potentially unprofessional request," he said. "It's just a last-ditch effort. I need...something. Whatever it is that I've been doing isn't working."

"What is it that you have been doing?"

Taken aback once more, Arlo searched for words that would expose him to the least amount of vulnerability while still getting the point across.

"I just thought that if I took care of her and gave her a stable environment, her memory would slowly return and our life would go back to the way it was." He shrugged sadly. "In some ways it's worked—she can make new memories and name people in old photographs now. But she memorized those names. She still wouldn't recognize anyone on the street."

The expression on Arlo's face reminded Hanne of a kitten she'd once had. The animal had broken its leg and did not understand why one of its appendages was suddenly encased in a plaster cylinder. It would drag the cast around, attempting to leap from chair to desk to bookcase just as it had always done, but it would inevitably fall clumsily to the ground. It would try again, and again, and again, until eventually it would give up and curl into a ball under the bed. For the second time that day Hanne clutched the edges of her bench with white knuckles to steady herself, only this time in response to the overpowering surge of tenderness that had suddenly flooded her entire body.

"Take three spritzes in each nostril," Hanne instructed. "Bend over when you do it, like this." She demonstrated, pitching her body forward at the waist. Her hair brushed against Arlo's arm. It felt satiny, like doll hair.

Arlo insufflated the compound from a green bottle that Hanne produced from her pocket. Even before he had finished inhaling the last spritz, the floor beneath him changed from speckled white rubber into a shining opalescent mirror marred by shoe scuffs. Until then he had never noticed how many different kinds of soles had left their marks on the floor, as if to give instructions to future scientists on the proper way to dance around the space.

As he straightened himself into a standing position, Arlo felt hyperaware of the commanding presence of machinery in the lab. He could hear every bubble in the cytometer, every whirr of a centrifuge, every individual hum of a freezer. He even thought he could hear the scuffles of the mice in their cages several rooms away.

"Are you all right?"

Hanne's voice, on the other hand, seemed far away. Arlo turned toward her and the rest of the room receded into space as if on warp drive. Hanne's coat was the color of concrete on a hot day when the air bends above it, her hair the cyan of sulfur fire.

"It's hot in here," Arlo said.

"Yes, you are sweating. Let's get you some water," she said.

Gold coins poured out of Hanne's mouth as she spoke. Arlo obediently followed her down the deserted hallway.

Several hours later, Arlo walked home. The effect of the spray hadn't completely worn off, so he didn't want to risk driving. He felt wobbly and out of sorts. The mercurial evening light had ebbed from gold to grey, and the world was cast in moody tones. He questioned how he usually held his face when he walked. Did he look at the ground? Did he smile at passersby? People seemed overly curious and sinister. How much did he normally lift his feet when he walked?

Overall, Arlo thought, his life was not unfolding as predicted.

PART II

⋮   George scrubbed the cursor to the beginning of the AudioNote file. Of all the speeches Dr. Westing had ever
given, this was George's favorite. Making it the first
item in the dossier was a stroke of inspiration that had
come to him as he was falling asleep the night before.
He pressed play. Dr. Westing's voice came through the
small speakers under his desk, at once booming and
tinny.

*As brand creators and technologists, we are living in an
exciting time. Society is more variegated than ever, and a
new form of humanity lives among us. Indeed, a new form
of humanity lives because of us, though we have decided to
keep the facts of our contribution under our hat for now.
Let us all take a moment to truly digest the gravity of such
a position.*

Though our original idea failed, it resulted in an even greater opportunity for growth. Many of the people who have gone through the Casino's Roulette system have no past, and a questionable future. They are currently under assault from medical scientists who are hard at work trying to recover their old identities. As all of us in this room know, that is simply not going to work. Identity is not inherent: It is constructed and can be demolished just like a building. For the Ruga, the old identity has been obliterated. There is a vacuum in its place. A sparkling, new, rapidly growing market waiting for products to populate it with identity markers. Rarely are we handed such a blank book waiting to be written.

This is not to disparage the scientific paradigm. After all, scientists are our main source of secondary data in this uncharted market. From science we have learned, for example, that the Ruga are capable of hyperarousal at certain types of emotional stimuli. One of these is hunger. Causality has not been well established, however, and, now more than ever, primary market research is of utmost importance. We need to learn what the Ruga desire before those desires can be written for them by a competing firm.

Adoption in this market is a matter of placing the brand in line of sight at the right time and place. Over the last century, religion has all but disappeared from the lives of

Americans and people the world over. God has been dead since the advent of modernity. The last major victim of our culture's ruthless process of illusion shattering has been romantic love. We can see the negative impact this has made. People are crying out for something to worship. Why else would anyone willingly play a game as absurd and dangerous as Roulette? We, as brand creators, can make that holy thing that people are willing to go through hell to find. Can you think of a more necessary, a more compassionate work, than to create a deity?

This means, of course, amping up research efforts. Why should focus groups be cloistered in a room? Why shouldn't research be conducted in the exact context in which a religion would be practiced: normal, everyday life? Is it, in fact, a violation of privacy to record what people do in their daily lives, to commodify the daily experience? Is that not what artists and writers have done since the establishment of genre painting and the novel?

To acquire this kind of information effectively, we don't need facilitators. We need anthropologists. I retract that. We don't need academics at all. We need friends, lovers. And not just any lovers. For, as all of us in the room who work in the luxury market know, we do not seduce our targets but dominate them.

Considering that he had awoken to the steady shiver of rain against the bay windows, and especially considering that he had somehow pulled a calf muscle in his sleep, Arlo felt not unhappy that morning. Though the softness of the bed and Mara's warm, sweaty body were not easy to leave behind, Arlo expected that the rest of his day would be smoothly embroidered with activity as if under the staccato needle of a sewing machine. He let his mind wander while he brushed his teeth.

Arlo and Mara had watched a movie the night before about a man who was wedded to the wild, having abandoned his children for a life of roasting animal carcasses deep in the snowy wilderness over beds of hot coals. He was a classically trained chef who had become feral. The movie seemed to portray him as an icon of freedom. Arlo had accidentally smoked too much marijuana before the movie in an attempt to replace the effects of the OAN spray with a more familiar intoxication. The combination of substances had magnified the scope of that freedom to mythological proportions. There were slow-motion scenes of fire and ash flying through the air, of vegetables roasting seductively in their skin. The man's beard was white like a god's. Outwardly, Arlo had expressed disapproval that such a person would choose to have children.

"What an asshole. People like this are so selfish."

Mara, also incredibly high, had nodded in agreement. They both wondered privately if they would ever have children.

A presentation for the Life-Extension Gala awaited completion on Arlo's laptop. He stared at the screen, not really seeing it. It was the bright pink port wine stain on Hanne's chest that he was thinking about. She usually kept it hidden under slim turtlenecks, but the flash of it as he worked her crewneck sweater over her head in the cold storage room the evening before had overwhelmed him. He had kissed her there expecting to taste berries.

After they both came, they sat on the ground leaning against the giant orbital shaker, allowing its hypnotic motion to spread the warm glow of post-orgasmic prolactin throughout their bodies. Arlo felt insulated and cozy despite the chill of the cold storage unit making the hairs on his arms stand on end. Hanne was talking about how she had decided to go back to school in her early thirties because she felt that it was time for her to do something good in the world. She had studied art in undergrad because she did not understand its purpose and expected that getting a degree in the thing would make it clear. Unfortunately, her education had only served to confuse her further. Over many years and after a period of prolonged depression, she'd had to accept that there were emotions and motivations in the world that she would never have access to, and that instead of trying to recreate them for herself, she needed to simply accept the reality of their absence in her life—for the sake of her own sanity. She turned her mind to science, where purposes were much clearer.

It was raining harder now. Arlo suddenly remembered that the only time he had ever prayed to god was when he was a child at a sleepover with a friend who missed his mother so much that he couldn't stop crying. Arlo had prayed for his friend's mother to come back, but she didn't. Eventually the friend fell asleep in the soggy marsh of his teary pillow. They never talked about that night. Arlo felt guilty that he had seen his friend in such a weakened state, but also secretly felt closer to him.

In a similar way, his sense of shame for cheating on Mara was overshadowed by the intimacy he felt with himself, as if he'd finally had an experience that he could truly call his own. He did not—or chose not to—remember at that moment how Hanne's crescendoing expirations as she came were flung at him with a peculiar sense of urgency, containing the stunned realization of something unfairly imprisoned that had finally been set free.

———

The Life-Extension Gala was a study in literality. Tables lined in holographic tiles emitted blue and green and lavender arcs of light into the ballroom air. Crushed velvet napkins gleamed like mylar. Pale pink and mauve tea roses, clustered in crystal vases, occupied the center of the table and stood in for the heads of those seated opposite Mara, whose pinky finger brushed a gold fork and noted its expensive inertia. Waiters in Italian tuxedos swiveled around gala attendees in cashmere sweat suits and silk gowns who were discussing the effectiveness of blood transfusions from children in order to maintain youthful vigor into the sixth decade of life.

Mara tried not to notice that Arlo was looking at Hanne, whose long neck craned over a charcuterie spread like a snowy egret poised for a dive. The sinuous lines of Hanne's simple linen shift cut her form into precise segments of black and white. Mara felt her face twitching uncontrollably and considered burying her head inside the pink milk-glass bowl of strawberry ice cream on the dessert table. Instead, she turned away and concentrated on the citrus branches and peonies arrested mid-bloom inside the ten-foot-tall blocks of ice that had been placed around the dance floor. A presenter was saying something onstage.

Our methods are straightforward: blast the rats with excessive information for seconds at a time. Sound, light, touch, taste, smell. The results are remarkable. Despite forgetting simple things like how to run a maze they've run hundreds of times before, the rats live longer. Nearly twice as long, in fact. These experiments show that the dissolution of memory may be necessary at specific intervals for the prolongation of life. Here to tell us more about this fascinating work is the lead researcher—

At the exact moment that Arlo smiled at Hanne as he made his way up to the stage, the experience of jealousy jogged something so singularly familiar inside of Mara that she—in a sensation she thought she had lost forever—noticed the small yet unmistakable presence of her own soul.

———

After some deliberation, Arlo decided to bring Mara to the Life-Extension Gala. Her presence would be an adequate lance to drain any cysts of professional gossip that might be forming in the lab as a result of his encounter with Hanne. Mara's recovery was going well enough that as long as she didn't become mired in any kind of real conversation, no one would recognize that there was anything wrong with her at all. And she would hardly be the only one there with a fabricated past. Arlo glanced at his coworkers. Beautiful and well-compensated companions of various genders stood majestically among his more squirrely colleagues, making small talk and eating canapés.

There were a few married couples among the elderly attendees. After its romantic pretensions had been shot to hell by economic analysts, marriage had been re-branded as a luxury product, the aging legal bond lending historicity to the couple in the way a buttery, expensive leather does to a handbag. Though they were not yet married, Arlo felt that he had spent too long tending to the fabric of his life with Mara to just discard it. As for her illness, doesn't the burl growing monstrously on the body of a tree eventually impart a rippling beauty to the credenza formed from it? Like a malignant burl, his predicament was an honest one: it couldn't be reproduced just for the sake of aesthetics.

Arlo, who in the guise of taking in the scene had been

watching Hanne's fingers investigate slices of spicy capicola, shifted his attention to the brightly lit stage just in time to hear the presenter call his name. There was a cascade of applause. He fished for his notes and walked resolutely toward the stage, flashing Hanne a tight-lipped smile as he passed her. When he turned around to face the audience, he noticed under the dim neon lights illuminating the audience that Mara's face had turned into a fleshy and impossible staircase.

———

Earlier that night, Hanne had glanced in the rearview mirror as she pulled her car into the parking lot. She glugged a small bottle of vodka that she kept in the glove compartment and applied a slick of lip gloss. Just because she would be alone at a formal work function in the presence of a coworker whom she had recently fucked in a freezer didn't mean that she couldn't at least try to have a good time.

Twenty minutes later, Hanne saw Arlo enter the ballroom, looking elegant in an olive-green suit. Mara was attached to his elbow wearing the strangest dress that Hanne had ever seen. It appeared to be made from peach-colored cellophane with only density of material strategically obscuring the body underneath. The dress was ruched arbitrarily, with enormous triangular sleeves and a stiff, angular skirt. It made her look like a trapezoid with limbs. Long, palladium-colored curls frizzed around her face.

Guests tried not to stare as the couple walked into the hall. Mara's dress let out bursts of crepitations like a bag of potato chips. A digging motion near Hanne's sternum alerted her to an approaching dysphoria. She watched it advance as she once did a tornado during a holiday in Enghien. It had a similar snaking quality and brought the same assurance of misery—either her own or someone else's. Though she knew the walls of this twister were just the debris of her own ego, its violent churning threatened to level whatever structures of stable personality she had managed to erect. During times like this, she found solace in cheese, of which there were mercifully many varieties to choose from at the event.

Later, from the corner of her eye, Hanne watched Mara's face pleat into a mathematical impossibility at the sight of her own. Hanne felt a stabbing pain in her stomach. Its intensity nearly made her double over. She left the ballroom and tried to calm herself in the parking lot. She took several spritzes of nasal spray, lit a cigarette, and put her headphones in. She would try to listen to the radio until the feeling passed.

A sad song. Then a commercial.

You love the city, but is it aging you? Over the last fifty years, Dr. Frank Darlington has been a pioneer of excellence in plastic surgery, specializing in techniques that relax facial tissues rendered hypertonic from the accumulated stressors of modern urban living. Research shows that visual exposure to poverty, income inequality, and disease—all common on city streets—causes psychological stress that manifests in fine lines and wrinkles.

Filthy city streets cause disgust and contempt, emotions that are expressed through the nasal dilator and the levator labii superioris alaeque nasi muscles. Overactivation of these muscles causes deep, unsightly furrows of the nasolabial folds and contributes to snoring. Dr. Darlington's patented technique not only removes these furrows but also addresses negative emotions like guilt, shame, and revulsion, which are commonly associated with urban living.

Double-blind studies as well as patient self-reporting show a striking reduction in wrinkles and distressing emotions, along with increased quality of life, after implementation of Dr. Darlington's patented technique. Dr. Darlington also specializes in removing Ruga modifications, dissolving varicose veins, and addressing other cosmetic complaints of a vascular nature. Come to our downtown office today for a complimentary consultation.

Hanne peered at her reflection in a car window and touched the beginning of a small furrow that was forming between her eyebrows. After choosing not to undergo Ruga surgery, she had learned to live with the dysphoria and debilitating gastrointestinal pain of post-Roulette life. But she had never gotten over the fear that wrinkles appearing over the normal course of aging would one day illuminate her face with the story of who she really was. With the cigarette dangling from her lips she kneaded the crease while tucking a wayward strand of hair back into place with her other hand.

———

On the drive home from the gala, Mara's tiny sleeping body engulfed in the iridescent folds of her dress reminded Arlo of *Xerces blue*, an extinct butterfly. He could only see her when the sparse orange streetlights flashed over her crumpled shape. Her existence there in the front seat of the car was a mere flicker.

Arlo carried Mara to bed. When he tried to help her out of her dress she fought back sleepily. Arlo tucked the covers over the crinkling mound of fabric and turned off the lights. An old bottle of whiskey he had been saving for a special occasion was the only alcohol in the house, so he poured some in a glass and scrolled through streams of social media.

Someone had posted a video of a tsunami breaching the levee of a Japanese coastal town. It didn't look menacing or monstrous like a lightning strike or structure fire. The water simply spilled over the barrier, languid and unrelenting and infinite. It washed away cars on the street like pieces of trash, transforming into a river of metal as it approached the town.

The video had been shot by a person standing with a group of others at the top of a tall building perhaps half a mile from the wall. Their voices didn't sound angry, upset, or even scared. The translations at the bottom of the screen showed that they were repeating the same phrase over and over again.

What Is Happening

What Is Happening

Arlo remembered that when she was well, Mara had once probed, carefully, into why Arlo never complimented her appearance.

"I don't?" he had responded. "I feel like I do."

"You don't," she said. "But it's okay. I just wonder whether you notice things like that."

"Of course I do," Arlo said.

"So why don't you say anything?"

"I just don't feel the need to, I guess," he said.

The issue would come up again several times during later conflicts, but Arlo was never sure how it related to the problem at hand.

"I don't understand," he would say. "What does that have to do with anything?"

Mara would cry, her sadness spilling over some abstract barrier of camaraderie between them.

Afterward, Arlo would try in earnest to compliment Mara, but the words came out wooden. It was awkward for everyone involved.

———

Mara walked through Chinatown and paid three dollars for beef and rice porridge. She loaded it with hot oil and looked at a book of pencil drawings made by an artist with ataxia. The lines shuddered. Then she went to the thrift store, where she saw an elderly Chinese woman examining a terra-cotta monkey.

"That's an interesting statue," Mara said.

"This red monkey here is my mother." The woman's

exquisitely sun-wrinkled face crumpled like tinfoil. She was the oldest Ruga person Mara had seen. Mara's face crumpled like tissue paper in response. They looked at each other for some time. "Would you like to come to my house and have some tea?"

The woman, whose name was Bea, lived in a single-room occupancy in a senior residence facility, on the fifth floor of a massive Italian Neo-Renaissance-style building that had once been a grand hotel. Chinese women wearing pastel nylon tracksuits, their thinning grey hair cut into chic bobs, were deep in conversation on worn-out velvet chairs in the grand lobby. An Out of Order sign was taped to the brushed brass elevator door.

"A night heron somehow got into the elevator shaft," Bea explained. "Its body was ground into the machinery. They're removing it bone by bone."

They climbed five flights of worn carpeted stairs to Bea's room. The old woman's gait was stooped but steady. Bewildering shapes came into focus as Bea unlocked the door to her home, which appeared to be a life-size diorama designed by a child with a flair for horror. Mysterious objects littered the room, arranged with inscrutable intention.

"The ancients used this method to memorize epic

poems," Bea said as she led Mara through the cramped space. "You place an object in a room and attach it to something you'd like to remember. You can build a life this way."

Mara vaguely recognized this method. "Isn't it supposed to be an internal map?"

"I can't remember internal maps," Bea said in a way that conveyed *duh*. She shuffled her feet out of her outside shoes and into paper-thin grey flannel slippers.

"The kitchen is my childhood," Bea said as she boiled water for tea, "and the living room is my present." The kitchen was littered with statues of monkeys of various compositions and colors. The living room, with cats. Mara examined a statue of a white cat inside of a well-seasoned wok on the living room floor.

"The cats represent my husband, and the wok is our favorite restaurant," explained Bea. "When I see the cat in the wok, it reminds me that last week, I went out to eat with my husband and I had a nice time. He does not want to live with me anymore."

Mara nodded. "I have a system kind of like this too, but mine is more compact."

Bea poured boiling water over a nylon satchel of tea leaves in a milk-glass cup. Mara marveled at the thicket of objects. Here was a glass terrarium with a tortoiseshell inside. A zinnia-colored wooden wolf. A Sugar Babies wrapper arranged just so in a slice of sunlight.

"Sorry about the mess," Bea said, dexterously picking up the wrapper with her toes still in the slippers and throwing it in the trash bin.

"Do you ever get rid of things?"

"Sometimes I make the memories I don't want or need anymore into new ones. But usually it's forced." Bea's face fell. "The residence workers come in and throw away this and that. To them it looks like I'm hoarding trash. I don't know how to explain that these objects are important to me."

The Casino was visible from Bea's window. Its name was printed on the blue sky like the Hollywood sign. Bea's face held up to the afternoon light resembled the curled petals of a chrysanthemum. She was saying something about her past. Photons like invisible bees pollinated impressions from Bea's face to Mara's, which through a noumenal mechanism synthesized its own dermal array. A corpus callosum of gaze integrated two wrinkled catalogues of experiences and beings into one moment of indulgent, luxurious grasping. It was headier than wine, Mara found, and though it contained all the qualities of sex—immediacy, mental and physical stimulation, a mysterious and ancient logic, levity, love—it was a sensation exceptionally distinct from anything else she had ever felt.

———

Mara left Bea's house and walked back to her own. The glitching noise of malfunctioning electric church bells thickened the air. Simultaneously, a voice broke into *adhan* from the loudspeaker of a neighboring mosque. Prayer is better than sleep, it said. Both buildings were in disrepair.

Mara entered her bedroom and closed the door. Sun-bleached curtains were drawn across the bay windows, letting in a small amount of light that bathed the room in a calm, dark glow. Mara flipped the light switch on, overpowering the glow and throwing the creases on the curtains into relief. She sat down on the floor.

Here was a floorboard that no longer squeaked because Arlo had spent a weekend fixing it while Mara tossed and turned in fever. When she had to go to the bathroom, he'd carried her to the toilet and helped her wipe. He'd spent hours with her writing down the memories she had left so that she could look back upon them if her condition worsened.

Realizing she was having difficulty reading, he then offered to record them into audio, but Mara had declined.

"It doesn't matter," she said.

"It matters very much," he responded.

Some people grow steadily, like a tree. Others are like volcanic rock, the accumulated sediment of serial eruptions. Arlo was an analog vine creeping along the violently digital protrusion of her existence. He had maintained the edifice of their life together even as it crumbled. Like a faithful fresco restorer, he never tried to impose his own will or interpretations in his care of her. Sitting on the floor, Mara despaired at this. Becoming oneself took more energy than she could muster alone. If Arlo would only draw a picture of her, or write a summary, or even make a crude joke about who she was, or used to be. But Arlo did not make representations. He only searched and researched and preserved.

Mara thought about being an old woman like Bea. She thought about her own silver hair and Bea's and Hanne's, and the way Hanne had flinched when she saw Arlo at the gala. Mara recognized the quality of that flinch. It contained the horror of fingernails clawing at a room purposefully made without a door.

She noted again the presence of her soul dressed as jealousy.

Mara got up and went to the closet, where she pulled out her mandala trees. Several were tangled together and expanded springily like a metal tumbleweed. Far from being things that she could use to reach Arlo, the spiny assemblies had become dense and inscrutable even to her.

Dressed as a wombat at a Halloween lawn party several months before taking the action that would come to define her life, Mara had overheard Arlo talking to Li about an attractive friend they had in common. The discussion was very brief and very benign, with Arlo only commenting on the brightness of the friend's eyes. There was a reddish tint to his assessment.

It had shattered the hope in Mara that perhaps certain feelings simply didn't happen to Arlo. The drunker she got that night, the more she felt a sinking certainty that she would never hear the words "you are beautiful" spoken by a man she loved ever again. The loss of this vision of romantic love drained Mara's body of the holy, so she drank a rather dangerous amount of vodka and passed out at nine o'clock in a plastic lawn chair, looking at the moon.

The smothering grief had dissipated by the next

morning, replaced by a cruel hangover. But it returned with newfound vigor some days later, rendering Mara immobile in bed. Millions of notions of who she could become surged through her body with unbearable alacrity while opportunities to actually be anything at all seemed to slide through her fingers each moment like slip clay. She had become pure subjectivity, formless and invisible, an annoying almost-presence obsessed with the act of *describing*. She diagnosed herself as incapable of either inspiring or creating due to a terminal indeterminacy.

Mara stopped putting on makeup. She was tired of suggesting ways for people to view her. Polishing the surfaces of her face only gave off the mistaken impression that there was a "her" to view at all. She stopped putting on clothes and bundled herself under blankets instead. The demarcating forces of sunlight, water, soaps, and lotions all became far removed from her increasingly translucent skin, pushing her further into abstraction. Arlo was worried but chalked it up to the depression that occurs after one abandons an old life for a new one.

Holding the mandala trees sparked a memory of a moon in Mara, who tried to keep it cupped in her hand like a captured moth.

On the night that Mara left, Arlo dreamt of a boulevard lined with yellow trees. The dream was occupied by thoughts about the unbearable substance of trees—the way their branches might touch you without permission; their audacity in growing into a million tongues that rustled at the slightest provocation, a constant protest that formed the background hum of life (for those who could still afford to live near trees). The trees lining the dream boulevard had leaves that were yellow dollar bills and rustled with the sound of the inside of a wallet.

By the time Arlo woke up from this dream, the day was already ripe and smelled faintly of pears. He felt the conspicuous absence of Mara's body as one would feel the sudden inability to speak.

He sat up in bed and swung his feet to the wooden floor. That existed, at least. Standing up was not so successful. Arlo's head swam and he fell backward into bed, where he lay without thoughts, without feelings, with barely any consciousness whatsoever, for what felt like several hours. In reality it was twenty-three minutes. After those twenty-three minutes, Arlo managed to get up and put on a pair of jeans that he'd fished out of the laundry hamper; a white polo shirt;

and a black sweater. He rumpled his hair in front of the mirror as if he were someone who could see his own reflection and have opinions about it. Grabbing his backpack from a chair, he walked out of his front door without locking it behind him. The rain had washed away the particulates from the air and he could see the hills around him in perfect clarity. The world was beautiful. He noted again that the day smelled of pears.

The vast research campus looked devoid of life at 10:50 a.m. The buildings consumed and regurgitated bodies on a tightly fixed schedule here. He scanned his ID tag on the magnet strip and walked through the green glass doors of his building.

The security guard looked up and nodded. "G'morning. Oversleep?"

Arlo ignored him and hit the elevator button several times. The security guard frowned. This was not behavior characteristic of Arlo.

"You all right?"

Arlo entered the elevator and hit the fourth-floor button repeatedly until the doors closed. The security guard wondered what was up but was not able to pursue the train of thought very far, as he then saw several pigeons attack the lunch buffet laid out by visiting pharmaceutical representatives in the atrium of the building. The rest of the security guard's morning was spent chasing birds away from sandwiches.

Arlo spent the entire day in the rodent holding room watching the mice in their plastic containers. He tried not to think about where Mara was. She would return shortly. She could not take care of herself. She had no money. She loved him. Each sick or lost animal also meant the loss of years of life and millions of fleeting acts of devotion. It was embarrassing and frustrating when things like this happened, and it seemed to Arlo that they were happening more frequently.

———

George closed the recording of Dr. Westing's speech and connected an even older external hard drive to the computer. Though he missed the elder Westing's vision, he had to admit that despite—or perhaps because of—his lack of talent, Westing Jr. had an endearing innocence that made him flexible enough to know when to give in.

Scrolling farther and farther back into the archives, George clicked open an AudioNote file time-stamped over three decades ago. The thing that began it all. He scrubbed the cursor to the beginning and pressed play. He recognized his own voice, young and hesitant, spilling from the small speakers. He had no idea then of the ways that his first talk as an engineer in the R&D wing of an emerging technologies company would change the trajectory of his life.

Good afternoon. Thank you, Dr. Westing, for the generous introduction. I am honored to have known Dr. Westing since our days in the navy, which we both left around the same time to begin work on the current project. So . . . let's jump right in.

The total womenswear retail market has decreased steadily over the past decade thanks to continued stagnation in average consumer incomes and per capita spending power. Online retailing has been significant in adding impetus for growth in the market while at the same time increasing the costs of operating brick-and-mortar storefronts. In this talk, I will present an argument for why physical storefronts present a radically new opportunity for growth.

Consumers are becoming more sophisticated and individualistic. Increasingly they suffer from image-fatigue, leading many to purge advertisements from their lives altogether. One image that can never be purged, however, is the image of the self.

Clothing doesn't simply reflect identity—it creates it.

This was the basis for forays into augmented-reality

dressing rooms that allowed consumers to see themselves in the clothes as they would be seen in real life. A leather jacket doesn't look quite the same in a dressing room as it does in a mosh pit. However, at first the quality of the environmental graphics was low and the imagery itself uninspired. After several high-profile boutiques rolled out the feature with disappointing results, the idea was abandoned as a nonviable gimmick.

However, recent advances in the science of memory visualization may allow us to create a dressing room that not only surrounds the consumer in a lifelike environment relevant to her tastes but indeed constructs this environment by pulling archetypal images from her own memories. While this proposition is in itself profound, we may even go one step further and suggest that by manipulating the proprioception of the consumer with EGO technology and inducing something similar to an out-of-body experience, we can allow her to view herself from a third-person vantage point for a complete and unified contemplation of the desired identity.

Scientific and anthropological literature suggests that autoscopic experiences stimulate a feeling of communion with divinity. While fashion has long employed religious imagery to sell clothing, it has never directly used the numinous to imprint itself into the psyche of the consumer. If *successful, this technology has the potential to change the way people think about the retail experience, as well as to reconceptualize the social purpose of apparel.*

George pressed pause on the AudioNote file at the sound of a knock at the front door.

———

George opened the door of a beige Victorian house dingy with mildew. Mara was embraced by the welcoming smell of chorizo and cheese.

"It smells amazing in here," said Mara.

"We've been cooking all morning—I don't even smell it anymore. Come on in," George said. They climbed a dark set of stairs to a landing filled with a tangle of rusted bicycles.

"How many people live here?" asked Mara.

"Ten of us, but sometimes more if friends need to crash," George said, smiling.

Whitewashed wooden crates, stacked from floor to ceiling, lined the hallway that led to the kitchen. A ladder leaned haphazardly to one side. Personal belongings overflowed from the crates. There were shoes and bits of fake fur and diapers, cookbooks and diaries and crystals, a basketball and a small popcorn machine. Despite the unreasonable number of objects in the hallway, the curious symmetry and balance of the crates made the whole thing look intentional.

Sudden sunlight seeped through the lace curtains at the kitchen window, illuminating a hanging garden of pots and pans drooping heavily from the ceiling. Spice jars and bottles of brownish-red liquids jostled each other in racks upon racks on the wall. A pot of macaroni and cheese peppered with red chili powder bubbled seductively on the stove.

Mara's eyes jumped from corner to corner and landed at last on the enormous kitchen table laden with boxes of nonperishable food. Dehydrated ice cream, steaks, seafood, and vegetables were stacked alongside the biggest variety of instant ramen that Mara had ever seen. Kimchi-flavored, spicy pot au feu, jalapeño chicken, shrimp tom yum. Individually wrapped packages of dried fruit and nuts from various airlines spilled out of a giant sugar waffle cone onto the wooden surface like a Thanksgiving cornucopia.

"That's our community table. We put all of our uneaten food there in case people get hungry," George said. "You're welcome to it, of course."

"Thank you," Mara said. "This is so generous."

"Anytime."

"So where is everyone?"

"Out back," George said, and opened the door to a tiny linoleum-floored room crammed with two sets of bunk beds and a plastic sink in one corner. It appeared to have been a laundry room at some point. They squeezed past dressers stacked on top of each other and stepped out into the backyard.

The evening sun filtered through fruit trees that canopied a group of people working on a massive sculpture, which sprawled throughout the enormous backyard. Metal bars crisscrossed between the trees, tied to the branches with rope. Pale teenagers were stretching strips of sheer white and orange silk over the metal bars and tying them in knots. The light that filtered through the silk cast on the ground colors difficult to name. A person with a shaved head and scars on their body was embroidering tiny mirrors onto the silk as another pushed beer cans through a small cement crucible that melted them down and ejected a pile of aluminum disks, which gleamed like treasure.

———

Mara sent a short message to Arlo telling him that she was all right but would like to be left alone, then switched off her phone permanently. For the next several weeks, she slept in an inflatable kayak in the hallway of George's house. Though there were many beings in the house, they remained more or less invisible to her. Once, she awoke to the roommate with the shaved head—Bean—sleepwalking in the hallway and urinating into the paper bag that contained her clothes. Mara wasn't sure whether to wake them up— she didn't want any sudden noises to turn the glittering arc in her direction.

"Bean pissed on my clothes last night," Mara told George.

"Did they?" George made a noise with his teeth. "They do that sometimes. I have a rack of clothes at work that I'm not using for staging anymore. Do you want some of those?"

"Sure, that'd be great," Mara said. "Will they fit me?"

"I think so, but it depends on how you like things to fit," George said. That evening, he brought back a brown shopping bag filled with snagged slip dresses and white button-down shirts with long French cuffs.

"If you have a job, why do you live with so many people?" Mara asked while setting the table for dinner one night.

"It's not really about me; I'm doing fine. But being Ruga can make it hard for some people to hold down a job."

Mara glanced outside at the group of people winding fabric around a tree. George had explained earlier that week that the sculpture was a form of political discourse that had been in progress for months. She was only beginning to understand the basics of its grammar.

"The housing crisis makes everything harder," George continued as he crowded the table settings closer together to make room for a few more. "Plus, I used to live in a submarine. I don't mind tight spaces."

Tall and heavyset, George had the serious air of a Buddha reincarnated as a navy vet. Every crease on him was perfectly pressed. He was careful and thorough in his explanations, if somewhat long-winded. Mara had heard him say many things over the days that she'd spent at his house, but none of it explained his anachronisms. Most discomfiting of all, he seemed to remember nearly everything of his life before Roulette. And though he explained this by the troves of recordings he kept for his work, if it weren't for the exceptionally coherent morphology of his expressions, Mara would have begun to doubt his authenticity. All in all, though she still didn't feel she knew him very

well, she'd begun to see George as a strong line of char-
coal on paper.

———

Spring arrived. The backyard burst into bloom: roses
of every color, everywhere. Vicious tiger lilies hatched
from bulbs buried deep underground; impression-
istic brushstrokes of white yarrow clustered within
green foliage. Then, in no time, summer bore down
with its explosion of lush stone-fruit trees and garlic.
Sunrise-colored peaches swelled in pneumatic formations on boughs that drooped under the weight of
their flesh. Molecules of each day passed through the
membrane of the next. Mara slept in the button-downs
and woke to stare through the kitchen window at the
leaves of the plum tree from her kayak. Every morning she wept in the kayak, though in some ways she felt
more at peace than ever.

"*Le diable bat sa femme et marie sa fille,*" George said
once as he walked by her in the hall. Outside, an unsta-
ble crow fell off a branch.

Sometimes she could hear George working in his
room. He would listen to the same audio files over and
over again. The walls between them garbled the content. Once when George was out, Mara peeked into his

room. It was littered with vintage electronics, pink and yellow carbon copies, watercolor paper awash with gradients, and an electronic keyboard. Mara picked up a yellow slip of paper: a handwritten tabulation of money spent on a shawarma wrap, beer, and gas. She turned it over.

INCIDENT REPORT: Last Sunday, July 27, was the first full human trial run of the Ruminous 2.0 prototype. Past tests have resulted in minimal issues—however, there was an incident during this trial that may warrant a temporary or permanent cessation of further human testing.

An error in the proprioceptive manipulation mechanism caused an over-dissociation of the subject's psyche, leading to severe memory loss. The subject was the lead in-house developer, who had volunteered for the position. Subsequent questioning revealed that though the desired state of aesthetic preoccupation had been achieved, there were undesirable side effects such as disorganized thoughts and identity confusion, which suggests that this hyper-augmented application of EGO technology is not ideal for the retail setting.

I have contacted Will Cunningham at the VA Hospital for therapeutic recommendations regarding the subject. Ruminous 2.0 prototype testing is suspended until further notice.

Incident Reported By: Kelly Liam

George set down a sculpture on his boss's table: an immense, turquoise, intestine-shaped mass shot through with burnt orange and red and gold. Its edges seemed to be shifting slightly in the way that a slug's body writhes under salt.

"What is this?" Westing Jr. asked.

"A 3-D visualization of a space-time tubeform data set. It's a proof of concept for the dossier that the data can be made legible to our instruments."

Westing Jr. stared at the structure. He thought he could see the shapes of two people copulating within it. He could almost hear them sighing. It made him nauseous.

"What kind of data?" During brief moments of self-consciousness, Westing Jr. worried that his employees were aware that he did not know anything.

"Sounds and images, mostly. Imagine very long and convoluted art films. We were able to extract thousands of these from the Roulette system. And in each, there are thousands of terabytes of data to sift through and sync up and project and tag and sculpt and whatnot.

Most is garbage. But there's some very valuable stuff in there. Stuff that could make the past several years of work all worth it. I'm going to need at least another graduate student to help me extract those."

Westing Jr. sighed loudly and pretended to massage his smooth brow while observing George's face through his fingers. Its habitually placid nature annoyed him. It's not like George wasn't well compensated. The least he could do was emote. And he happened to know for a fact that George did not lack emotions, having witnessed him silently laughing with another Ruga employee from across the room during a meeting. Though he could not be sure that what they were doing actually constituted laughter, the cadence of the ripples on their faces at the time seemed to indicate synchronized mirth, probably at his own expense.

Westing Jr. shivered as the intestinal people let out a distinct moan. George seemed to not have heard it. Perhaps his girlfriend was right in her assessment that he had been "an asshole" and had done too much cocaine the night before, Westing Jr. considered.

"I'm sure you realize that this is a major breakthrough. The trouble we've had in projecting archetypal imagery in Ruga users of the Ruminous 5.0

dressing rooms is due to their memory consolidation issues producing a fragmented sense of self—so much so that there's barely any identity scaffolding for us to hang garment imagery on. But I have an idea on how we can get around this, and I'd like to try an experiment," George said. "I need some time and resources to work out the technical kinks so we can present a prototype in the grant application."

"An experiment? I'm not sure we have time for experiments."

George seemed to hesitate. "Without overpromising, the gist of it is that I want to see if the Ruga will recognize archetypes associated with their old memories, with the eventual goal of productizing such imagery as part of the Ruminous experience."

Westing Jr. wanted to say something here about needing to keep costs of operations low but was unable to due to a bolus of some material trying to escape his throat through his mouth. Instead, he waved his hand as if to request more detail.

"The Ruga customer doesn't respond to advertising imagery as other consumers do because their lifetime stock of visual associations has been obliterated from the psyche. However, since the Casino records all data associated with each individual Roulette experience, a low-resolution version of each Ruga person is stored in the Casino's systems. My theory, informed somewhat by my own experiences, is that the object of desire for the Ruga individual is the prior self, and that productizing this self to the Ruga is our best bet going forward." George gazed at a framed picture sitting on the table of a large man holding a gummy baby. It was Dr. Westing holding Westing Jr. at age two. "It's a curious question. Do you think anyone recognizes the person they used to be?"

Westing Jr. was suddenly embarrassed at the infantile representation of himself and made a mental note to eliminate it from his office as soon as possible. "Fine," he said thickly, clearing his throat. "Get another student if you need to. And please tell Jordan to order me a Caesar salad on your way out."

George nodded and got up to leave.

"Don't forget your thing," Westing Jr. said, almost screaming.

———

Sparrows hopped arithmetically on the sidewalk. To sparrows, humans must look comically slow and bumbling, Mara thought. Whale-shaped clouds passed by overhead. To sparrows, whales must be timeless.

It was Saturday afternoon. George was taking Mara and a six-pack of nearly frozen beer to a warehouse in the industrial part of the city. Mara was running out of money and had taken George up on his offer to help him with some work. "Please keep this under your hat," he had said at the outset. "I wish I could offer everyone who needs it a job, but the truth of the matter is that there is an element of taste involved."

The city had a lonely temperature. Chicken wire houses with papier-mâché walls allowed winds to transgress the boundaries of comfort. In many neighborhoods, several families lived together in one house due to the intensifying housing crisis. People spilled from corner stores and bars into the streets and slept there at night, shitting near trees, or not near anything at all. Well-to-do parents posted angry fliers on the trees about the homelessness problem. *There are feces everywhere—enough is enough!* Yet no one could figure out how else things could be.

George and Mara walked past pendulous cranes that transferred shipping containers from barge to dock, delivering shipments of mysterious goods no one could afford. Enormous piles of refuse covered in black plastic sculpted the bay coastline like domes of cooled lava.

They stopped in front of a yellow building with red and black graffiti squiggled across the rusting door. George unlocked it and led Mara inside.

Glass windows gridded the loft from floor to ceiling; the afternoon sun flooded the space in a surreal glare. George set the beer down in a square of sunlight. The room was mostly empty except for an old piano atop a faded Persian rug. Next to the piano was a desk with a laptop and a crate of equipment spilling over with wires. The largest object in the room was a black box. It looked as if it had been carved from gleaming stone.

"What is that?" Mara asked, gesturing to the box.

"A dressing room," George said.

"A dressing room," Mara repeated.

"Do you want to try it?"

"What do you mean, try it? Are there clothes inside?"

"You'll see. Just go in the ones you're wearing. Take one of the white collared shirts from the bag over there and put it on when it feels right. Think of this as your first task on the job."

George opened a beer, sat down at the piano, and began to play an arpeggio. The instrument sounded warm and slightly out of tune, each key asymptotically reaching for its note.

Mara grabbed a white collared shirt and entered the box wearing the same clothes she had left her house in months ago: a black T-shirt that she'd taken from Arlo and faded black jeans. She touched the interior walls. They felt like diaphanous curtains. There were no discernable cameras.

The walls lit up slowly and for a moment became a mirror. Mara saw her own pale face staring back at her. She looked haggard, like a monk. Her fingers felt strange, like they needed something to press or hold or dig their nails into or they'd float away.

An image wrapped around the box. Rainbow lines and boxes filled the mirrored space like pipes from a vintage screensaver. Rows of triangles and circles lyrically dotted the walls, revealing patterns that probably made sense to someone somewhere. Mara looked around for a projector but did not see one.

The lines animated and zoomed around the box. Mara could make out a black-and-white human form underneath the racing lines. As it became clearer, she realized it was Arlo, but he was not wearing clothes that she recognized. He sat motionless in a thick, oatmeal-colored sweater and pleated wool pants on a stool in an empty room, eyes downturned at a screen. The vivid bones of his knuckles cradled the screen in his lap. Rainbow lines flowed across it like river rapids. Arlo looked cut out of a magazine.

Mara saw herself, wearing a black T-shirt and jeans, approaching Arlo. Suddenly, she couldn't move, realizing that her vantage point was located somewhere near the top of the box. Arlo glanced toward her approaching form with a cavernous expression. Who was operating her body if she was up here, Mara wondered. She saw herself look into Arlo's eyes with ferocity and walk straight toward him into the walls of the box. Their bodies smashed into each other in a massive swell and faded out, leaving only the hyperactive graphs in their wake. She watched the lines move around for some time while her body dropped back into itself. Once she felt fully integrated again, Mara buttoned up the white dress shirt over her T-shirt.

A new image wrapped around her. A dark woman with limp orange hair wearing a white dress shirt sat in a desk chair. From the woman's outstretched palm emerged a network of rectangular cells filled with pastel colors and formulas for carrying out simple operations. The walls were now covered in rippling lilac satin dripping puddles of molten gold onto the bare cement floor. The woman's eyes were downcast and her expression somber, as if processing the gravity of what she had unleashed.

The woman's face resembled her own, but the dips and valleys of the bones were more pronounced. Her eyes slightly larger, wider set. The skin flawless. Seeing a beautiful and alien version of herself somehow did not make Mara feel in the least bit surprised, or covetous, or much of anything. Instead, a feeling of great emptiness spread inward toward her eyes from her temples.

Mara walked out of the box. George had taken his shirt off and was playing "Moonlight Sonata" in the reticulated sunlight. Globes of sweat shone in the crevices of his dark body. It had gotten very hot in the loft.

"That was ... what was that?" Mara said.

George played the sonata more vigorously. "Did it make you want to buy clothes?"

"Sort of," Mara said.

George laughed.

"How does it work?"

"It's complicated."

"I have time. Was that the whole task?"

George shook his head and slowed his playing, blending the notes together with the pedal so they dropped like pigment on wet paper. "In the 1910s a woman named Perky did an experiment to see if people would be able to distinguish their mental images from images that were actually being projected on a screen."

Mara sat down on the cement ground with her legs splayed out in a comfortable position. She reached over and grabbed a can of beer. The tab made a fresh metallic sound as she snapped it open.

"The subjects were told to look at a blank wall and visualize a banana. The results showed that people thought their minds were producing the elongated yellow shape of a banana on the wall when it was actually a very faint image being back-projected by the researcher. This became known as the Perky Effect."

"Huh," Mara said. George continued to play, his hands moving across the keys like large brown spiders.

"The Perky Effect works best when people are relaxed, maybe flipping through a magazine. Pornography and fashion photography have relied on some version of this effect to sell magazines to people who automatically imagine themselves in the position of the models. Do you know anything about EGO therapy?"

Mara shook her head.

"It was originally developed to help people with body dysmorphia habituate to their own reflection. You hook someone with dysmorphia up to a distress recorder and put them in front of something that looks like a mirror but is actually a projector. First you project their true reflection, and based on their level of distress, you start manipulating the image imperceptibly toward the ideal in their head using deep neural network translation, until their distress diminishes to subthreshold levels. This reconstructed, idealized form becomes their baseline. Over the course of months, you allow the baseline to slowly revert back to the person's actual morphology. They don't notice and eventually get used to their own reflection. It was an eminently humane invention."

George slowed his playing even more until it was just an amber gloss over the afternoon light and turned to look at Mara.

"But like most humane inventions, it was perverted into a weapon. The fashion industry had faced pressure for a long time to expand its visual vocabulary of beauty but realized that doing so would undermine its ability to induce envy, one of the most potent motivators for purchasing. So it decided instead to change what people saw in the mirror to sell clothes.

"High-end shops had custom mirrors built using EGO that would make their clients look the way the clothes were *designed* to make them look. It was all very subtle, and all the more powerful for it. Back home their reflections returned to normal, leaving a craving for another glimpse at the idealized self and its associated clothing. Of course, there was an immediate outcry. Many people tried to explain why this was a bad idea. But no one listened. The mirrors are still around. Very difficult to distinguish from normal mirrors.

"I was young and full of ideas then. I didn't think it was ethical to fool people into thinking that a projected image was themselves. I wanted to turn the volume up a little bit, make it obvious that clothing is fantasy. But things break. Nothing turns out as expected. My goal was to show people how they saw themselves, but the universe butted in. I didn't want to open that box," George said, and rested a massive finger on a single note. C#.

Mara looked at George expectantly, waiting for him to finish his story, but he had stopped talking. The waves of the last C# dispersed for the rest of eternity into the air.

"I don't understand," Mara finally said.

"It's called Ruminous," George said, gesturing to the

black box. "It's my second try at introducing the public to the dressing room of the future. The first one was too . . . strong." His face undulated with implication.

Mara looked at the black box and back to George's face, which now appeared globe-like and greenish. He suddenly made a mechanical hissing noise with his teeth, the exact noise of a Roulette machine locking shut.

Mara gasped. Her face burst into innumerable shades of pink in comprehension as she realized why George had looked so familiar sitting at the bar that first afternoon: he was the smiling young scientist with the afro in the article she had seen in the Casino waiting room.

———

George sat motionless at the piano. Mara's face was a tessellation of affect. The infernal phrase *purposeful meaninglessness* flashed in her head as she wondered— for the very first time, she noted with surprise—what on earth George wanted from her. Why had he picked her for this job when he lived in a house brimming with people? Did all of them know who he was and what he had made? Additionally, did the fact that she recognized his face from a tiny, grainy image mean that her brain wasn't irreparably broken? Tremblingly Mara raised the can of beer to her lips.

"Did you recognize anything that you saw in the dressing room?" George asked gently, as if he could see now that he was dealing with a wounded animal.

Mara said nothing as her mind swam in a bog of dread, attempting to pull itself out by grasping onto the reeds of various paranoias.

"If you'd like to take another look at what you saw, you can," George said, gesturing to the laptop. "It's all recorded. Might be easier to analyze the second time around."

Mara shook her head as if she were trying to get water out of her ear. Her thoughts seemed stuck, like her leaden feet in nightmares of being chased by some unnameable terror. "What's recorded?" she asked thickly.

"The way it works is really not so different from EGO therapy for body dysmorphia, or from the original Ruminous dressing rooms that were based on it," George continued as if he hadn't heard her. "But instead of pulling images from your brain directly, the system is using images recorded during your time in the Roulette system. We already know that the Ruminous technology works for non-Ruga people, I'm just experimenting to see how it works for people like us."

"I'm sorry, but you just casually tell me that you basically invented Roulette, and now, now you're putting me in a box, showing me recordings of my own memories that I didn't even know existed? I don't—why are you doing this to me?"

George retracted his head into his neck like an affronted tortoise. "I thought you wanted a job. And, to a degree, I wanted you to be the first one to get back what you lost," he said. "I'm sorry."

"But why didn't you tell me about it?"

"Because I need your unbiased responses."

"So you just rummaged through my memories, my thoughts, my—" Mara's face shimmered with anger. She had stupidly considered George a comrade in a barren desert of irrelation.

"No, not your memories, necessarily," George said, moving his hand toward Mara's; she shrank away and he withdrew it. "Only what was recorded during your time in the Roulette. Who knows if the imagery produced in the system is even based on memories." He seemed genuinely hurt by Mara's reaction.

"So what did it show *you*?"

George looked away and twitched a shoulder.

Mara laughed derisively. "Let me see your data set, then," she said. "It's only fair. Since you know so much about me now."

"I consumed and deleted my data set a long time ago," George said quietly.

Mara considered throwing her can of beer at George's head. Why hadn't she ever stopped to wonder why George seemed so unaffected by being Ruga? She had taken his integration as evidence of strength of character. It was now clear that the way he looked at her, the way his face responded to hers, reflected nothing but the feeling one gets when looking at a distinctively colored bug under a magnifying glass. Her face burned.

"This technology is a threat to the Casino's future. It does something quite similar to the Roulette but in a way that doesn't destroy the mind." George had taken on the air of a beleaguered parent. "Not to mention the fact that it comes with an easy revenue stream. Can't you think of a single reason why I wouldn't want them to be able to access my data set?"

"But you were fine with them having the rest of ours." Mara brought the beer to her mouth and shakily took another sip. She recalled the reams of disclaimers and forms she'd had to sign before entering Roulette.

Though she didn't remember the details, Mara felt fairly certain that none of them indicated her memories might be used in retail advertising. But the problem with words—even very technical words—was how they slid meaning from one location to another at the behest of their interpreters. Like black ice. Mara considered asking George about the legality of his operation, but simply thinking about it exhausted her.

"Do you work for the Casino?"

"No. My boss sold the space-time tubeform algorithms I had accidentally discovered to the Casino when it became clear it was worth more to them than to us. Look, my eventual goal is to give the data sets back to the people they belong to. These dressing room advertisements are the only way I could get funding to even begin to do this. I'm asking for your help."

Mara scrutinized George's face for a hint as to whether he was telling the truth. It was completely expressionless, like the face of someone watching TV.

"Lie to me," Mara said. "I want to see something."

"What?"

"Just do it," Mara said. "Lie. I had to do it. With a needle stuck in my neck. It's not so hard."

"This statement is false," George said. His face pulled together and apart into Julia sets.

"A real lie."

"You are not beautiful," George said.

The wet can slipped from Mara's hand and sprayed beer all over the white button-up shirt, soaking her chest and face. Mara blushed violently and pawed at her eyes.

George began to laugh: an uproarious, belly-shaking laugh that normally delighted Mara in the way it sliced through his seriousness to reveal the soft, round egg-ness of him. But this time his laughter activated an expression in Mara that—despite knowing deep down it was nothing more complicated than garden-variety fury—George nevertheless interpreted in the way that would cause him the least amount of pain: the visceral longing of a person who no longer had anything left to protect.

———

The day before Hanne returned to Belgium, she stood at Arlo's empty bench and watched a hot water bath swirl chemicals around. Into it she quietly and with care expelled a globule of spit she had collected in her mouth for him.

Hanne's apartment was almost completely bare, but it still took her about five hours to pack. She found herself moving objects from one place to another in the apartment with no real purpose in mind. In the bathroom, she opened and closed the mirrored door of a cabinet several times before the contents came into focus. Tubes of creams and bottles of serums that she applied to her face to strip off dead skin lined the shelves. In a way she was always presenting a new, raw face to the world. Hanne thought about all the baby wrinkles she dissolved away each day, never giving them a chance to live.

Hanne scraped these bottles into a bag. She took an amphetamine to speed up time. Later she trimmed her bangs with enthusiasm. Hair had always been a good friend to her. Uncomplaining, compliant, amenable to being cut with blades. No one was going to put her in a hospital for cutting her hair. Hanne cried as she cut her bangs shorter and shorter, exposing her white eyebrows. In the airport, she vomited into a toilet.

Back in Belgium, Hanne noted some commotion. She looked out the window of her hostel room to see people mourning someone who had died. They were wearing white clothes and weeping with their heads resting on each other's shoulders. Hanne had gone to a town by herself where the only attractions were a hotel and a bar. The bar had a taxidermic polar bear. The hotel used to be a brothel. Hanne sat on a chair that belonged to a woman who used to work in the room and watched the candlelit procession stream past her window.

"I get it," she said aloud to the walls. "I understand, thank you, I get it."

—

Mara uncurled her fingers from George's wooly chest. The room was pitch black. Everyone else in the house was asleep. "George," she whispered. He didn't stir.

She carefully turned over in bed and searched the floor for a pair of raw denim jeans. They had been thrown onto the skeletal backrest of an ergonomic chair, where it lay stiffly crumpled. In the stain of moonlight seeping under the crack of the door Mara could just barely make out George's keys attached to a belt loop by a carabiner. She slid out of bed and put her clothes on, keeping a close eye on George, whose breath sounded like the low rumble of magma in a fitfully sleeping volcano. She unclipped his keys from his jeans and slipped out the door. In the hallway, she touched the inflatable kayak for the last time, leaving the few things she owned in the paper bag next to it.

Mara walked to the house she used to share with

Arlo. She let herself in silently and walked slowly through the small rooms of her old life. The faint luster of the moon mingled with the glow of a porch light through the kitchen window illuminated a thin film of dust that covered everything. Mara picked up a tin of coffee. It was difficult to move, as if affixed to the counter by a temporal syrup.

Mara walked into their bedroom where Arlo was sleeping and lightly caressed his arm.

Arlo awoke to something crawling on his arm. He kept his eyes closed and tried not to scream. This had happened once before, when Mara had woken him up by turning the lights on in their room.

"Wake up, Arlo, but don't scream," she had said.

Back then, he had opened his eyes and seen Beelzebub on his pillow. The opalescent, swollen corpse of a massive horsefly was broken open near his shoulder. A squirming mass of nearly translucent maggots had eaten their way out of their mother's body and were pulsating from the yellowing pillowcase onto Arlo's arms.

That was then. This time, there was no demon. It was only Mara.

"I'm sorry if I scared you," Mara said to Arlo. Arlo stared, disoriented. Mara's figure loomed over him: taller, firmer in her embodiment than ever before; paradoxically so, as if she had stepped out of a gash in the skin of a whiskey-soaked dream. "Come with me," she said urgently and extended a hand, which he took as if hypnotized.

They walked past the docks. A buoy bobbed in the black water under the moon. It was very late, but there was a child on a tricycle on the dock and there was a woman. The woman was smoking a cigarette, her face a pile of yarn. Arlo's scalp sparkled with a prodromal energy. He squeezed Mara's hand. She did not squeeze back but kept hurrying forward.

It took some time for Mara to find the right key to open the loft. Each key insisted upon itself only to dissolve into a mass of identical others. The right one finally appeared after a mysterious series of insertions, and the heavy door groaned as Mara pushed it open.

Arlo tried to push the mixture of intoxication and hangover that had come to define his nights and early mornings far enough into the background of his awareness to inspect his surroundings. Reflections off the asphalt-colored bay lit the cold loft in the palest shade of black. The moon made a square on the floor, but a passing cloud erased it. It was too dark to see much in the anemic light coming from the street. A strong, unfamiliar smell hung in the air. Bats, he supposed. Arlo wondered if this was where Mara had been living these past months and—as he allowed his mouth to be enveloped in hers—at what point he ought to ask what the hell was going on. The part of his pride that was injured that Mara had left him twice was temporarily wrestled into compliance by the part of it swelling with certainty that she would always come back to him, albeit transformed. Feeling ill, he decided to let himself be temporarily soothed.

The next several minutes unfolded rapidly. Both of them naked and shivering, Mara took Arlo's hand, walked into the dressing room, and sat down on the floor. Arlo sat next to her and pulled her close, though he sensed a coldness within her. He wanted to melt back into the familiar comfort of her body as he had done unthinkingly on so many nights.

The box was dark. A soft, shrill sound emanated from below them as the walls of the box became a mirror. They looked at their reflections alone and together, bodies knobby, skin the greyish color of a brain. Slowly, they felt themselves pulled toward the ceiling, detached from their own small forms huddled on that floor and surrounded by black masses, a peculiar landscape of stone. The mirror had become a sky the color of thought.

There was a sound. The sound came from all around: a metal bowl clattering, an abused theremin, a terrorized wildcat. Three hundred violins playing the same horrible note all at once and unceasingly. A wave of pleasure swept through Mara's body, immediately followed by one of sickness as the walls around her undulated like the view from a porthole. The system was attempting to integrate two perspectives into one.

Fleshy and improbable forms populated the walls of the dressing room. Young men with skin made of homemade paper, boys with eyes carved from sea glass, hands, joints, a finger stuck in the vacuum of pink puckered lips. Women with bodies perverted by some deranged development to contain more than their fair share of pleasurable bits interlocked in cartilaginous shapes, thrumming with indulgences. A morbid curiosity pinned Arlo's lids open, bathing the darting orbs of his eyes in a procreative and recreational phantasmagoria at once familiar and foreign.

The phantoms disappeared as the dressing room used up the stock of imagery it had drawn from Mara's

Roulette files. A distorted image of Hanne now loomed on the screen; a watercolor splash of pink under her naked collarbones flashed as she picked up a tube of meat and stuck it in her mouth in a lurid motion. The sound of violins had turned into that of droning machines chopped and glued together.

Mara's heart quickened. The dressing room was using EGO in real-time to reconstruct and modify images from Arlo's mind, all the while hurtling her toward dissolution. Through prickling eyes she forced herself to confront the truth: Hanne's ephemeral nude contours snaking up the machines of a lab. Once she had desired to be such a presence in Arlo's mind—a vision of beauty inhabiting its crevices and influencing its actions at a distance. In attempting to rid herself of this desire she had destroyed a delicate and powerful thing. Unknowingly, she had released into herself a solvent capable of dissolving its own container. But now that she was molten and liquescent, she could run within the veins of the densest rock.

The ends of Hanne's hair twinkled. Suddenly the walls of the dressing room transformed into an open night sky: the glittering wound of the Milky Way. Then, arabesques scintillated over scenes of nature's sublime: lenticular clouds over a mountain peak, a vast green gorge dissected by a river. Trees became the open faces of friends only to turn into rock formations under the high desert sun.

Mara then saw her own face, tinted in honey and rose. The walls zoomed out to show her as a dancer, whirling in ecstasy, hands forming mudras. She wore a garland of apple blossoms and night-blooming datura, the white thorn-apple. The music changed to a warm song with lyrics in an unintelligible language. Spinning Mara danced over an immense landscape, pounding mountains with red feet, ankles encased in bells.

Then a domestic scene. Though it simply depicted Arlo and Mara chatting over breakfast cereal at a dining table, this scene was the strangest of them all. The visual tone veered from depictions of domestic American bliss hailing from the age of the vacuum cleaner to intrusive close-ups of mouths and ears like in a perfume commercial. When the system finally landed on a visual style, it most closely resembled the dead formalism of overly symmetric movie sets. The effect was not attractive.

But Mara gulped down the images like a polydipsic in the throes of a lethal psychosis. It was her. She was the dancer, she was the one bursting into peals of laughter at the table, it was her body and her face that covered the walls of the dressing room. Arlo might occupy a mythological space in her own mind, but she was very much real and alive in his. Mara felt infused with a perverse sense of gratitude but also remorse and confusion. How much of what she was seeing came from Arlo, and how much from the machinations of the dressing room itself?

In her bewilderment, Mara did not notice that Arlo's body had stiffened and was convulsing against her own until the strobing walls no longer showed any images at all and static had replaced the sound of spoons clattering against china.

At first Mara thought that Arlo was weeping. But the sound of his body struggling to breathe between clenched teeth alerted her to a change in his physiologic state and she dropped back into her body with frightening immediacy. Mara dragged Arlo from the dressing room and crouched over his shuddering mass, frozen with terror. She had an uncertain understanding that there was no point in calling an ambulance for most seizures and furthermore lacked confidence that being found in his current situation would be beneficial to Arlo's health in the long term.

After several minutes, the convulsions slowed in intensity and duration and he began to breathe normally, eventually drifting into a deep and silent sleep. Flooded with relief, Mara felt a beastly fatigue descend upon her as well. She curled up next to Arlo on the floor, holding his pale, clammy body close to her own.

Everything was dark once more. Weak orange streetlights halfheartedly illuminated the walls of the loft. Something blue and shining flickered nearby for some time and then went out.

———

Arlo was naked and curled up on the floor of the loft, sunlight pouring through his curls. His hands were clasped around his knees. Mara could see all the minute ridges of his face—each and every one of the delicate bones. Sunlight glanced off the white tips of his blond eyelashes as they fluttered like moth's antennae in REM sleep.

Illuminated by the light of dawn, Arlo's body looked different than she remembered. Maybe he had lost weight during their separation, or maybe the expansiveness of the loft made him look smaller, more embryonic. He had not lost his glow, but she realized now that it was the sheen of sweat and sebum irregularly dispersed over his body and face. Some of it had solidified into waxy deposits near his nose and behind his earlobes. The cups of his eyelids were marbled with delicate lavender vessels. One corner of his mouth was pooling with drool.

A small pebble was embedded in Mara's cheek where she had pressed against it all night on the cold concrete floor. She lifted her head and winced in pain as a muscle spasm sent a shock wave down her right shoulder. In an attempt to slice through the fog of awakening, she tried to recall how she had ended up where she was. The shape of the full event occupied her memory as a hulking caniform, but as she honed in on specifics, the details scattered like cockroaches under bright light. All that came to mind was the shimmering blue light of the laptop lulling her toward deep slumber. The blue was gone now, replaced by the sleeping machine's winking green eye, which appeared to be a hundred yards away. Mara took it all in with her nose wrinkled and a pattern spreading across her face like puzzle pieces strewn across a table.

After managing to extract herself from the tangle of limbs without disturbing Arlo, Mara clicked the laptop awake. A blue screen appeared, with a new file timestamped 03:14 AM. Opening the file on the holographic display, she watched shining apparitions appear and disappear like summer rain for the second time that morning. The puzzle pieces of Mara's face moved closer and closer to each other until they disappeared altogether, leaving in their stead an expression of tranquility mixed with something else.

Mara wanted the file containing all that she had seen in the dressing room for herself. She wanted to keep Arlo's visions in a locket close to her breast like a precious lock of hair from a dead child, so that whenever she doubted her reality, she could clutch it and feel that she existed in at least one other place. Her nakedness becoming suddenly apparent to her, she pulled her clothes back on and rummaged through the crate of electronics for any external drives. She found only one: a small, nose-shaped amulet.

A breeze carried the sounds of the early morning dock through a crack between the window panes. The city was waking up. Mara felt her time with the machine running out by the progression of a sudden humidity—if she wanted to take something from it, she would have to choose quickly.

She found a folder marked RLT_RAW_DATA. Opening it revealed oceans of pasts in incomprehensible code. On a hunch, Mara searched her own name and found hundreds of associated files containing complicated instructions for opening and reading. It would take ages to sift through them all. As she looked at the sizes of the files, Mara also realized that the drive would fit less than half of her Roulette files, or the entirety of Arlo's constructed imagery from the dressing room. What it would not fit was both.

A dying plant cowered in a corner, its once-lovely fronds crumpling as if in apology. The bead-like body of a spider descended unhurriedly from the rafters. A dog was barking somewhere nearby. A cloud passing over the early sun made Arlo's comma-shaped form flicker for a nanosecond. Mara got a strange feeling. Her fingers tingled the same way they had in the dressing room.

While the files she needed transferred to the drive, Mara shook her hands vigorously until her fingertips grew bright with blood coursing under the skin.

Arlo's form no longer flickered. He now lay eerily still, as if cut from marble. Mara reached out and touched his face lightly. It was very warm and slightly sticky. Arlo's eyes opened, hazel irises completely engulfed by black pupils. They darted from side to side as he struggled to focus on the face before him.

"Hi," Mara said, smiling. "It's only me."

Early Monday morning, riot police responded to reports of the mass looting of foodstuffs from grocery retailers around the city. The perpetrators appeared to belong to the subculture known as Ruga. Due to striking facial modifications, the individuals are difficult to identify on security cameras. Looters wearing bandanas covering their faces may have been non-Ruga associates or anarchists. Ruga activists are calling the incident an inverted hunger strike.

"When the state sees a person purposefully starving as a political statement, it feeds them by force. But when it sees us dying from hunger on the streets due to poverty, it does nothing," said Bean, a Ruga activist. "It is clear that the state's main function is to violate the body and keep it weakened. The entire Ruga community feels excruciating pain when one of us starves, and we can't stand it anymore. We are exercising our right to food."

The government has grown increasingly intolerant of Ruga direct action in the face of the community's mass defection as research subjects from federally sponsored programs.

"The Ruga should have no reason to go hungry," Paolo Hernandez, the incumbent mayor of the city, posted on Twitter. "They have the amazing opportunity to support

themselves through federal funds by participating in research that expands our understanding of what it means to be human. What other group of people can claim such an honor?" The tweets continued, claiming that "the sudden and devastating exodus of Ruga from research programs that have been in progress for decades is an assault on science."

In response, Bean tweeted, somewhat cryptically: "We are not inert."

Mara was at the hair salon. A jewelry ad followed the news report on a sleek television screen. A woman with the auricle of one ear sheathed in gold was apparently caught up in some kind of romantic entanglement with a man who was all luminous eyes. Mara cringed in recognition of the nonoperational desire but could not help grinning in spite of herself. The ad was very realistic. The woman sitting in the leather chair opposite her was also looking at the screen, though whatever she was seeing seemed to shock her. Her lips were parted, eyebrows raised in the distinct gasp of a dog that had detected itself in a mirror for the very first time.

Many advertisements were now individualized to the viewer by means of retinal scanning, yet archetypal enough that they could be discussed with others. *That crimson dress is so beautiful, the way it flounces*—this could be said, and pointed to, and agreed or disagreed with, even its particularities referred to, without the acknowledgement or even understanding that each person had seen a slightly—sometimes entirely—different version of the product. Even during the infrequent instances when these differences were acknowledged, it was more common to privately suppose that the other person was unskilled at description than to consider that the percepts themselves differed. And of course, the less alike the ads that were seen, the less alike were the consumers seeing them, and the less likely they would be to have a conversation about it at all. This was becoming an unremarkable aspect of daily life.

The model on the screen turned to reveal her other ear, studded with a large crystal. Over the past year, Mara had gathered from the tailored ads that the self she'd chosen to discard had been particularly fond of minerals and their crystalline formalities. She now preferred cabochons of opals, glass, porcelain. Blurred, milky particles colloidally suspended forever in some foreign body. But despite the strangeness of being followed around by a digital ghost, she was thankful for the memories that her former advertising profile held onto. It made her feel safe.

"Thank you for waiting. We're finally ready for you," said a smiling stylist in a white cotton smock as she held out a cup of tea toward Mara.

Stopping at a red light on her way home— she was finally able to drive again—Mara ran her fingers through her freshly styled hair. It had been cut to chin-length and flattened into a lustrous platinum sheet. She pulled into her driveway and rubbed rose cream blush onto the apples of her cheeks. Her wan olive features suddenly looked alive with the shifting, iridophoric gleam of a cuttlefish.

Arlo looked up from the kitchen sink, where he was scrubbing dirt off of meaty, apricot-colored chanterelles. Mara hung her coat on a wall hook, revealing a simple black linen shift dress underneath.

"Your hair looks nice," Arlo said with a hint of surprise. This was a new look for Mara, but for reasons he couldn't quite put his finger on, she looked so oddly familiar. Maybe he had seen it in a magazine somewhere.

"Thank you," Mara said, smiling. Her cheeks shone mimetically in the colors of fruit from the family *rosaceae*, face wriggling into shapes of worms reconstituting the dead.

She could tell he meant it.

Acknowledgments

This book would not have been possible without the patient and generous guidance of my editor, Christine Neulieb, nor without the encouraging words offered by those who read early drafts. Finally, I would like to thank the past versions of myself, whom I hope to get to know better one day.

About the Author

Born in Kolkata, Jayinee Basu is the author of a book of poems entitled *Asuras* (Civil Coping Mechanisms 2014) and the English translator of Sukumar Ray's *HJBRL*. She has aided research on neurodegenerative disorders and traumatic brain injury, and is currently a second-year medical student at Touro University. She lives with her fiancé and cat in Oakland, CA.